# Definitely **Not** Camelot

Sequel to the award-winning novel, ****Posing as Ashley***

"Ashley's fight for confidence and peace with herself is nuanced and genuine ..." – *Children's Literature**

"... an immediately likeable protagonist whose desperate need to try to always please everyone else will resonate with many readers." – *CM: Canadian Review of Materials**

Published by Lobster Press™
1620 Sherbrooke Street West, Suites C & D
Montréal, Québec H3H 1C9
Tel. (514) 904-1100 • Fax (514) 904-1101 • www.lobsterpress.com

Publisher: Alison Fripp
Editorial Directors: Meghan Nolan & Mahak Jain
Editor: Shiran Teitelbaum
Editorial Assistants: Katherine Mason & Stephanie Campbell
Graphic Design & Production: Tammy Desnoyers
Production Assistant: Elena Blanco Moleón

We acknowledge the financial support of the Government of Canada through the Canada Book Fund for our publishing activities.

Library and Archives Canada Cataloguing in Publication

Peters, Kimberly Joy, 1969-
Definitely not Camelot / Kimberly Joy Peters.

Sequel to: Posing as Ashley.
ISBN 978-1-897550-63-2

I. Title.

PS8631.E823D43 2010 jC813'.6 C2009-905723-9



Printed and bound in Canada.

Text is printed on 100% recycled post-consumer fibre.

*In memory of my father.*

– Kimberly Joy Peters

# Definitely **Not** Camelot

written by
**Kimberly Joy Peters**

Lobster Press ™

# CHAPTER 1

Some people believe that things always turn out the way they are meant to, or that fate and circumstance intersect at a predetermined time and place to define our destinies.

Other people think we make our own luck, good or bad, and that everything that happens in our lives is ultimately up to us.

I think the answer lies somewhere in between.

* * *

In theory, I could have been forgiven if I'd gone into the eleventh grade anticipating nothing but the worst. After all, my mother had cancer, my boyfriend had dumped me, and I'd just walked out on a lucrative modeling contract because I'd disagreed with the agency's ethics. But as the school year began, I believed things would get better, and I was ready to do everything in my power to make it my best year ever.

On the first day back to classes, my mind was on my mother's chemotherapy, scheduled to begin that afternoon. Yet, it seemed as if everyone at school was talking about two things: my breakup with Brandon and my fledgling modeling career.

The comments began almost as soon as I found my new locker.

Cory, a guy I knew from the Algebra class I took last year, whistled and started rummaging through his backpack when he saw me. "Hey, Ashley!" he said, passing me a copy of an article. "Do me a favor and autograph this, will you? So my idiot cousin will believe me that I know you?"

"I'm hardly autograph-worthy!" I laughed, pushing the paper back. "Why don't you just show him the yearbook?"

"Because – no offense here – yearbook photos are yearbook photos, and nobody looks good in those. But *these* are kind of hot," he said, still waving the paper at me. "And you're probably the only professional model I'll ever know." I couldn't help but blush, and was relieved when Allie, whose locker was beside mine, joined the conversation.

"I think it's so cool that you signed with an agency, Ashley," she said, wide-eyed. "I mean, last year you were just like everyone else – except that you were joined at the lips to Brandon. But this year, you're a big model, and you're single, so you can totally enjoy it."

At the mention of the word "single," Cory raised his eyebrows. "Really?"

"Ashley and Brandon broke up right at the beginning of the summer. How could you *not* know that? There was so much discussion about it on E-Me after Brandon changed his relationship status."

"I was away at my uncle's cabin all summer," Cory said. "No Internet. I might have come home sooner if I'd known you were single, though," he winked at me. I tried to smile back, but Allie could tell something was wrong.

"Oh my gosh – you don't want to talk about the breakup. I am SO sorry!" she said as she covered her mouth with her hand.

It wasn't that I was still wallowing in self-pity or yearning to have Brandon back, although we'd been together for two years and I naively thought we'd last forever. Since we'd split up, Brandon and I had worked on our friendship, and I'd even had a brief rebound romance at a modeling convention over the summer.

But it was weird not to be with Brandon on the first day back at school. When I'd seen him in the hallway, I'd wanted to talk to him about how long my mom had spent on her makeup that morning while getting ready for her first chemo session. He would have understood because we used to joke all the time about how the house could be burning down and my mom would still want to comb her hair and put on lipstick before fleeing. But Brandon had been surrounded by a bunch of girls, and I didn't want to be the girl who just couldn't leave her ex alone.

From the way that he'd caught my eye and nodded only slightly before returning to his conversation with some blonde, I was pretty sure that he also felt the need for us to establish our non-couple identities. And if he was fielding as many post-breakup questions as I was – which was likely, as he'd left for camp just after it had happened – I knew he didn't need me adding to the rumors.

It was the gossip, not the breakup, that bugged me. The idea that other people had spent the summer posting comments about my love life (or lack thereof) on E-Me made me feel queasy. It was kind of like my high school's version of *The National Enquirer* or *Entertainment Tonight* – but in this case, at my expense.

"It's okay," I said to Allie and Cory. "Like you said, I'm single now, and I'm looking forward to a really great year."

"That's totally the right attitude," Allie said. Then she peered at the article over Cory's shoulder. "This might be a dumb question, but I couldn't really tell from the article – have you actually, like, had any real gigs yet? Or is it just like, you've got a contract with the agency and now you still have to wait to see if anyone thinks you're good enough to model for them?"

"I actually ended up quitting shortly after I signed," I explained. "Which is why I don't really think I should be autographing that article. I'm not really modeling anymore."

Allie's mouth dropped open far enough for me to see that she was chewing grape bubble gum, while Cory snapped his mouth shut.

In truth, I hadn't yet figured out whether I was going to stop modeling *completely*, or just put it on hold for a bit. My dad's girlfriend, Gabriella, had suggested I get into the business, and modeling had sounded like a lot of fun. But soon I'd realized how catty and competitive it really was. Then, I was asked to model fur-trimmed sweaters. As an animal lover and (hopefully) future veterinarian, I couldn't stomach the idea, so I'd walked away from the job.

When I quit, I didn't know if I'd ever be asked to model again. Some of my friends and family members had initially been disappointed, but I discovered that the ones who knew me best respected my decision.

Maybe I should have explained all of this to Allie and

Cory right then, but the bell rang just as they both asked, "How come?"

So I kept it simple and said, "I just didn't feel comfortable with some of the things they were asking me to do." I figured that this way, there wouldn't be as much room for discussion or E-Me debate about the horrors – or merits – of modeling fur.

By lunchtime, though, I'd had to say the same thing several times over, and I realized that keeping it simple might actually be harder than explaining everything.

"You're causing quite a buzz around here!" my best friend Caitlyn said as she joined me at lunch. "A lot of people are talking about your modeling career."

"I know," I acknowledged, looking down at my sandwich and exhaling heavily. "But they get awfully quiet when I tell them I quit."

Caitlyn continued filling me in on what she'd heard. "There's also lots of talk about you and Brandon," she said, shaking her head. "I totally thought your breakup would have been old news by now."

"Me too," I said, unwrapping my cheese sandwich, but suddenly not feeling hungry.

"So, have you talked to him today?" Caitlyn asked gently, looking up at me through her strawberry-blond bangs.

I shook my head. "We'll be fine." I smiled a bit, thinking about the little nod he'd given me when we'd made eye contact in the hall.

Caitlyn nodded in agreement, and asked me about the rest of my morning.

"Dad texted to say that Mom started her treatment. He snuck a *Playgirl* into her magazines, so we're just waiting for the fallout," I reported.

We laughed for a minute, imagining what my mom's reaction would be when she found a magazine full of naked men tucked between her *Forbes Weekly* and *Better Homes and Gardens*.

"Okay," Caitlyn gasped when we'd stopped giggling. "What else happened this morning?"

I fidgeted with the lid from Caitlyn's water bottle, and then I brought up the other thing that had been on my mind all morning. "I talked to Madame Galipeau before French class, and told her I can't go to Quebec."

In a case of Murphy's Law, I'd been scheduled to go on a French exchange to the province of Quebec for almost all of the first semester. I'd *really* wanted to go ever since I'd started learning French. But when I originally signed up for the program, at the end of tenth grade, my mom had just been diagnosed with breast cancer.

I was hoping surgery and radiation would have cured her by the end of the summer, so at the time, I didn't think going away in September would be an issue. But by August, the doctors were saying she needed more aggressive treatment. Obviously, I couldn't leave my mom during such a stressful time. Things might have been different if my parents had still been together, but they've been divorced for years. Despite Mom's insistence that she'd be okay, there was no way I would have enjoyed myself knowing she was home alone and sick.

Plus, the exchange was supposed to be reciprocal – my Quebecois hostess was supposed to come and stay with me during the second semester to learn English. And as much as I didn't want to think about it, I knew that if the chemo didn't work the way we hoped, having another girl stay at my mom's house later in the year might not be a good idea.

Reluctantly, I'd explained all of this to Madame Galipeau that morning. I didn't want her to make the "pity face" I usually got when people heard about my mom, but I had to give her reasons for canceling on such short notice. To my relief, she'd simply told me that she was sorry, and then started focusing on the logistics of me backing out.

"Madame Galipeau was pretty good about it," I told Caitlyn. "She said she was going to let the other school know that they'd have to make other arrangements for Mireille, my exchange partner."

I did my best to pronounce the girl's name as *Meer-ay*, with the fancy rolling "r" that Madame Galipeau had used, and that I'd been trying to perfect since I'd started taking French.

I watched Caitlyn's face carefully as I said it, and saw her smile. "*Mireille* – what a beautiful name!" she said, doing a pretty good job of rolling the "r" herself. "It makes me think of someone bubbly and adventurous."

"That's exactly what I thought," I confessed. "And then I felt like I was ruining her exchange opportunity by dropping out. It's supposed to be such a great program." I hesitated for a second before continuing. "Which is why I think you should go in my place."

At first, she looked at me as if I'd lost my mind. She squished up her nose, the way she does when she's thinking. And what I *hoped* she was thinking was that the idea wasn't actually as crazy as it sounded. Caitlyn had considered signing up for the exchange when I applied, but at the time, she was still getting over a really bad relationship, and her parents were keeping a super-close eye on her. Plus, her mom had just had a baby that spring, and I think maybe a part of Caitlyn didn't want to leave the new little sister she was just getting to know. But she'd had a great summer, and now I was the one whose family needed me. I just knew it was going to be an amazing experience, and I couldn't think of anyone who deserved it more than her. It made perfect sense for her to go and have a great time in my place.

"I don't know," she hesitated, pressing her lips together, but I could already see that she was considering it. I hadn't even started giving her all of the reasons I wanted her to do it, like how I just knew that her raw artistic talent would take her to Paris someday to work and to study history's great artists. If she improved her French now, it could give her a lot of future opportunities.

"The *only* thing holding me back is my mom's chemo-therapy," I reminded her in support of my position. "You'll still get all your credits, and you'll come back practically bilingual." Then, remembering that Caitlyn was more skilled than I was at balancing reason and emotion, I appealed to her heart and to her artistic sensibilities. "Caitlyn, it's going to be amazing. Quebec is supposed to be breathtakingly beautiful. Conner's going to be there too. I don't want to let Mireille down, and you've got a second chance to go."

"It would be so much better if we could *both* go. But

I guess I could talk to my mom about it," she said, tucking a strand of hair back behind her ear. "But I'd miss you, and I'd feel guilty leaving you here while I go away and have the great time you've been counting on."

I knew then that I had her.

"I'll be okay," I reassured her, squeezing her hand. "You won't miss me as much as you expect, because you'll be there with Conner."

Conner was Caitlyn's "un-boyfriend." To everyone who asked, they insisted they were just friends, but to anyone with eyes, their body language said otherwise. Conner was also artsy, and the two of them had worked together on a children's craft program over the summer. Having him with her in Quebec would be perfect.

Just as I said his name, he joined us at our table.

"Hey," he said, dropping a lunch tray on the table and smiling at Caitlyn. I noticed that he'd changed his hair color again, this time to black, with a streak of deep plum that highlighted his silver earrings. "What's up?"

"I'm trying to talk Caitlyn into taking my place on the Quebec exchange," I said, believing that he'd encourage her to go along.

"Spur-of-the-moment change of plans?" he said, tilting his head to one side and smiling at her again. "How very *Jackson Pollock* of you."

I rested my head on my arm in mock agony. Conner and Caitlyn play this game where they describe things with brush strokes and paint colors and other stuff they've learned in fine arts. It's usually cute, but this time, I had no idea what he was talking about. And I couldn't spoil their moment by asking for an explanation, because Caitlyn had put up with a lot of cutesy behavior and inside jokes when Brandon and I had been an item. I wasn't actually annoyed, but it did make me realize how different the year was going to be without them, and without my ex-boyfriend.

Caitlyn found Conner's joke funny enough to blush and giggle a little bit before he suddenly got serious.

"I think it's terrific, but Mrs. Van der Straeten is going to be *very* disappointed in you," he said.

"How come?" I butted in, wanting to know what their art teacher had to do with the French exchange.

"The drama department is doing *Camelot* this year, and I told her this morning that I'd paint scenery," Caitlyn said. Before I could tell her that I was sure they'd be okay without her (which would have been a total lie, because Caitlyn and Conner are the two best artists at school), she leaned forward. "Which makes me think," she said, "that since *you've* talked *me* into trying something new, I should talk *you* into something new as well."

I eyed her suspiciously and took a swig of juice while she continued.

"You should try out for the play." She leaned back triumphantly and popped a grape into her mouth, as if daring me to argue with her.

"Because?" I motioned with my hand for her to continue.

She shrugged. "Because you said you wanted to try new things this year, because you'll be able to meet new people while I'm away, and because you have a really nice singing voice. Besides, modeling and acting aren't all that different," she explained, itemizing her reasons as I'd just done with her.

Just then, my cell buzzed with a text message from Dad.

> Don't want to panic you, but try to hurry home after school, okay?

And just like that, all of my aspirations to try new things suddenly seemed trivial and unimportant.

# CHAPTER 2

Dad's car was in the driveway when I got home, so I crossed my fingers, hoping that it wasn't a bad sign. But before I could even drop my backpack at the front door, I realized from the sounds upstairs that he had stayed because the chemo's side effects had already hit. Mom was puking in the bathroom.

I'd wanted to go along to the hospital with her for that first chemo treatment, because we didn't know how it was going to affect her. But Mom – who'd had perfect attendance in high school and never let me forget it – wouldn't let me miss school even for this. Instead, my dad took her in for her appointment, and then brought her home.

Having my Dad there all day during the treatment, trying to make her laugh, might not have seemed unusual except that my parents have been divorced since I was four. My mom had remarried (and re-divorced) twice since Dad.

And now my dad was finally getting serious about someone else – Gabriella – for the first time since they'd split. It wasn't your typical family scenario, but I thought it was pretty cool how they had worked it out not just for my sake, but also to support each other. I think their maturity made it easier for me to get past my own anger with Brandon after our breakup.

"Is it as bad as we expected?" I whispered to Dad, hugging him.

"A bit worse," he said. "This is very hard on her, you know. She's not normally a barfer, so she doesn't have much patience for it." He smiled weakly at his own joke, as if Mom could control her nausea the way she controlled everything else in her life.

"I know," I replied. Though she had always nursed me through the stomach flu when I was little, I'd never actually seen *her* throw up. Obviously, I was aware that barfing was a possible consequence of chemotheraphy, but for a major control freak, Mom really surprised me by how little she actually wanted to know in advance about the treatments and their potential side effects.

*I* wasn't the one in treatment, but *I* still wanted to know everything about it. Her "let's wait and see" attitude unsettled me as much as it seemed to soothe her.

"If someone tells me the treatments will make me lightheaded, then I'm going to panic when I feel that way," she'd once said, "even if it's just because the room itself is too warm. It will be better if I don't know what might happen. Then I won't end up imagining symptoms."

I was surprised to hear her talk like that. My mom had been her usual, practical self all through her cancer diagnosis, surgery, and radiation. But something shifted when she'd learned she needed chemo. She'd always been like me – or I was like *her* – wanting to be in control, wanting to be prepared.

So when we found out she needed chemo, I did a lot of research. I started online, where I found all kinds of information and patient-support sites. Then I borrowed books from the library: optimistic titles like *CanSURVIVE!* and serious ones like *When the Worst Happens: Coping with Cancer* ... and funny ones like *Take These Breasts and Love Them!* I also tried to read all of the patient information leaflets my mom had brought home from the doctor's office. But I was kind of surprised that she had tossed some of them out – she was determined not to know what lay ahead.

She continued to tell me that I should feel free to come to her with any questions or concerns. But I didn't really see how she could answer them when she wasn't doing any of her own research. Plus, it was obvious that talking about it was still hard for her.

Case in point: the night before school started, I bought a bag of pink M&M's, the proceeds of which were supposed to go to breast cancer research. When I gave it to my mom, you'd have thought I'd offered her toad tongues.

"What are *these*?" she almost shrieked.

"They're for you," I said. "Your *Patients' Guide to Chemotherapy* says you can use a few extra calories before starting your treatments. I figured this might be a good time to start supporting the cause."

"Honey, I know you mean well," she replied. "But I don't want everything in my life to be about breast cancer. I'm a person – not an illness. And I don't need a bag of pink candy to remind me that I'm sick."

I held my tongue and took the candy back to my room, knowing that she had a good point. It was true that our lives shouldn't be *all about her cancer*, but it still felt like, for the moment, they already were.

Now, just one day later, she was on her knees with her head in the toilet. And despite all of my reading, there wasn't much I could do to help.

I hovered around Dad, bringing water and cold

compresses until Mom was able to find her way off the bathroom floor and back to bed.

Then, I offered her a couple of NausGone tablets I'd picked up at the health food store. "Try these," I said, reaching for a glass of water to help her wash them down. "They're supposed to help with the nausea."

She shook her head. "The doctor already gave me Gravol. I don't think I should mix drugs."

"But it's not a pharmaceutical," I insisted. "It's all natural – just some herbs and things. I read about it on the message boards of some reputable cancer-support websites. People swear by it."

She took a few sips to wash down the tablets, set the cup down on the bed tray, and then, sick as she was, asked about my first day of classes. "So how was it?"

Despite the nausea, she was still clearly in denial, so it didn't surprise me that she wanted to hear more about what was going on in my life.

"The usual first-day-back stuff," I said, hugging her. She wasn't as soft as she used to be. She seemed thinner, fragile, and I was almost afraid I'd squeeze her too tightly.

I knew we all needed more details than "the usual" to take our minds off her nausea, so I tried to come up with something I thought would interest her. "Most of the kids saw the article about my modeling. That gave them something to obsess about. Somebody even asked for an autograph. It was kind of flattering."

"I'm glad it went over all right," Dad said. "I know you were dreading their reactions."

"How was seeing Brandon?" Mom asked.

"Fine, mostly," I said, picking up our cat, Raven, and stroking her head. "It was weird not having lunch with him and everything. And there were a couple of nosy questions about why we weren't together anymore. But it was okay."

"That's great, sweetheart," she said as she bolted out of bed and back to the toilet.

Dad stayed for a few more hours, until Mom could rest a bit between trips to the bathroom. Being sick was still horrible for her, but compared to the constant throwing up she'd done during the first few hours after I'd come home, it felt like we were making progress.

"Are you sure you'll be okay?" Dad asked me for what seemed like the hundredth time before finally leaving.

I glanced toward my mom's bedroom door, and stood a little straighter before reassuring him. "We'll be fine."

"Okay," he smiled. "I'm sure Daphne must be getting desperate for a walk by now."

Daphne was my golden retriever, but since Mom was

allergic to her, she lived with my dad.

Usually, I alternated between Mom and Dad's place every fourth day. For the time being, though, Dad had agreed to let me stay with Mom during her treatments.

I planned to have dinner with Dad a few times a week and to walk Daphne as much as I could, even though I wasn't spending the night there. Like everything else that was going on, it wasn't perfect, but I'd always been good at balancing my commitments, so I believed I could make this work too.

"Call me if you need *anything*," Dad said, hugging me tightly.

"I will," I told him. "Love you."

It wasn't until after he'd left, with Mom sleeping and the house quiet, that I realized I hadn't eaten anything since lunch. We'd both tried to plan ahead for my mom's treatments, so there were all kinds of single-serving frozen meals I could heat up. But nothing seemed appealing. I was also reluctant to cook anything that might stink up the house and make my mom more nauseated. As I stared into the refrigerator, I suddenly remembered the M&M's.

They were on my desk, in their pink packaging, right where I'd left them. I opened them carefully and popped a couple into my mouth, letting them melt slowly while I went online. It was late, but I wanted to be *sure* Mom was okay. Plus, I hadn't been sleeping well for a couple of weeks, so staying up later seemed like a good way to make sure I'd sleep soundly after I did go to bed.

First, I did some more research on natural remedies, because whatever they'd given my mom at the hospital clearly hadn't worked (although the NausGone did seem to have helped somewhat). *Maybe we could try ginger tea,* I thought. Raven hopped onto my lap and I scratched her head as I checked message boards and patient advocacy sites for things that had helped other people get through their chemo experiences.

I'd become interested in natural products ever since one of my science teachers explained that a lot of medications were originally based on things in nature. For instance, chemicals from willow trees ultimately gave us aspirin. And roots that used to cause miscarriages were eventually turned into drugs that could induce labor.

I also knew from my earlier reading that chemotherapy works by poisoning your whole body, but cancer cells can't recover quite as quickly as normal cells. It's really like a war. There are going to be massive casualties on both sides, but to win it you have to kill more of the bad guys than the good guys. The result is a really toxic mix of stuff in your body that your liver has to flush out. With all of that going on inside of her, it was no wonder my mom was sick and retching. And I didn't think she needed any more artificially manufactured chemicals in her body, so I wanted her to try some herbal alternatives for the nausea and other side effects.

But there was only so much I could do at that hour, so I gave in to the urge to check my E-Me. Caitlyn wasn't online, but she'd updated her status to **Caitlyn is going to Quebec!!!** If I hadn't been worried about waking my mom, I would have squealed with excitement. Instead, I contented myself with whispering the good news into Raven's ear.

It was too late to call Caitlyn. But I sent her a quick message congratulating her on her new travel plans. Then I worked on updating my own E-Me status.

# CHAPTER 3

It seemed like everyone I knew had already updated their E-Me pages with comments about their first day back at school. But I wasn't sure what to put for mine.

I still had mixed feelings about the whole E-Me thing. I liked it when people wrote about their lives, like Caitlyn's Quebec announcement (well, it *would* have been news had it not been my idea). But I hated the gossipy stuff, and sometimes I just didn't get why some people posted the stuff they did. A girl I met at the modeling convention had just posted **Raquel is going to brush her teeth.** Nothing embarrassing or inappropriate, but not really interesting, except maybe to her dentist or the next person she'd be kissing.

I was pretty sure my *own* dentist wouldn't have approved of all the M&M's I was eating, but it wasn't as if I did it all the time. Besides which, the cat was purring so happily on my lap, I didn't have the heart to disturb her by going in search for something more nutritious. I popped a few more candies into my mouth while I considered what to post.

As satisfying as the M&Ms were, I wasn't prepared to go public with **Ashley is having chocolate for dinner** because A) I wasn't sure anyone would care about that any more than I cared about Raquel's oral hygiene, B) It sounded decadent if you didn't know the reasons *why* I was having chocolate, and C) It was kind of pathetic if you knew it was related to my barfing mother. And **Ashley's mother is a serial puker** didn't sound right, either.

I hadn't told a lot of people about my mom, and I'd decided that I wouldn't if I didn't have to. Partly, this was because my mother was such a private person. She'd told very few people about the cancer at the time of her surgery and radiation, and had only just begun discussing the chemo with other people.

But the biggest problem with telling people was exactly what I'd experienced with my French teacher. I didn't want people feeling sorry for me. Mom was going to get through the cancer. But there was also the issue of Brandon and me, and questions about why I wasn't modeling anymore. I didn't want to be "The Girl who has Everything Bad Happen to Her." I wanted to be "Ashley:

The Girl Who had an Amazing Year."

So in a lot of ways, as much as I didn't like reading the unimaginative updates, I completely understood why they were the most common. It's easy to write something that nobody cares about. It's hard to write something that matters. At least, it is for someone like me. I was raised by a mother who wasn't big on emotional outbursts, and who valued appearance and control almost as much as she valued her own well-being.

Finally, I decided to stop thinking so hard about doing everything perfectly and just typed. I settled on **Ashley wants to try new things this year.**

Almost immediately, a guy I knew from school posted, **Is that why you broke up with Brandon?**

I chuckled quietly at his quick thinking, and then amended my status: **Ashley wants to try new things this year - but still loves the classics like M&M's.**

Not profound, but honest, because by then I'd finished the entire bag of candy.

The cat shifted in my lap, flicking her ears at the sound of retching coming from down the hall. I was embarrassed to realize that for a few minutes, I'd actually managed to forget everything that was troubling me.

I know my mom made several more trips to the

bathroom that night because I was awake to hear them. Once again, despite having stayed up until well past two in the morning, I didn't sleep very well at all.

By morning, I was exhausted and my head was pounding, but Mom insisted that I go to school, reminding me that I couldn't do anything for her anyway. "Don't worry about me," she said from her spot on the bathroom floor. "Your dad's going to check on me, and I'm not very good company right now anyway." Then she reached out and rubbed my arm reassuringly, in a way that made me think *I* should have been doing it for her, and added, "Besides, I think one of us ought to make the day count for something. You only get to be sixteen once. Don't let *my* problems ruin *your* year."

I was still thinking about her words after school as I signed up to audition for *Camelot*. Although I'd never been in one of the school's musical productions before, I knew they took a lot of time. I already volunteered regularly at the animal shelter, and I knew I needed to pick up a bit more slack at home. But with my French exchange canceled, and Caitlyn going away, a musical seemed like the perfect chance to try something different.

It wasn't quite late enough to eat when I got home, but I stuck my head into Mom's room to check on her, and asked if she might want dinner.

"I had some ice chips a couple of hours ago," she said, shaking her head. "I managed to keep them down, but I don't have an appetite for anything else." My excitement at the prospect of telling her I had signed up for the musical quickly dissipated as I realized that she didn't want me to do things for her.

"You have to keep up your strength," I encouraged.

"Thank you, *Dr. Ashley*," she said, trying to remind me that she didn't want to know what she *needed* to do. But I couldn't stop trying to entice her.

"How about if I make some homemade macaroni and cheese?"

She smiled weakly and shook her head. "No thanks," she said. "*You're* still having dinner, though, right?" she asked, giving me a reassuring glimpse of the mother I was used to.

"Later," I said, figuring I'd heat up some of the lasagna Caitlyn's mom had dropped off. I sat down on her bed.

"Do you think the NausGone helped at all?" I asked. "I mean, did you feel any better today?"

She shrugged and held out her arms for me to hug her. "Not sure," she said. "But this is just what the doctor ordered. And I'll feel even better when you tell me about everything going on with you. I've been so out of it for the past three days that it feels like ages since we've talked."

The depth of *her* concern over *my* well-being made it hard to keep my voice light and easy.

"I went to Drama Club after school to sign up for the musical," I said as I sat down beside her and rearranged her covers. "It's *Camelot*."

"Oh, I *love Camelot*!" she said wistfully. "It's so full of hope and romance."

"Do you think so?" I asked. Even with no makeup and her long hair tied back, my mom looked beautiful. "The blurb they gave us said it was about a betrayal that caused the downfall of an idyllic kingdom. I thought it sounded kind of, well, sad." I traced my fingers over the flowers on her sheets, while Mom reached out and tucked a strand of hair behind my ear.

"Well, I don't want to give anything away if you haven't read it yet, but it's not *all* bad. A lot of it is really wonderful. I'd love to see you in it."

I'd heard of *Camelot* and of most of its main characters – King Arthur, Queen Guinevere, Sir Lancelot, and Merlin – but I didn't know much about the plot. I didn't actually read the full description or download the music until later that night. But sitting with her on her bed, thinking about a time in the future when she'd be well enough to come see me perform, was the moment I fell in love with the idea of being a part of the play.

After my mom had gone to sleep again, I began to review the audition notes and the story in detail. There was only one female speaking part – Queen Guinevere. I decided that that was the role I wanted.

The information sheet said that we could try out with a song of our choice, but I didn't think it would do me any good to audition by singing a pop song or a Christmas carol only to find out later that I didn't have the right range for the actual musical numbers. So instead of just going with a personal favorite, I decided to prepare a song that Guinevere would actually sing in the show.

I'd been to enough go-sees – modeling job auditions – that I didn't have a lot of concerns about the acting. And, as Caitlyn had pointed out, in a lot of ways, modeling really *was* like acting. Despite Caitlyn's assurances about my voice, though, I'd never considered myself a singer. And I'd never sung a solo. I thought I could hold my own in the shower or in a car with the music turned way up, but I'd also watched enough reality television to know that most people couldn't really gauge their own level of talent. So, with that in mind, I figured the best way to prepare for my tryout was the same way I'd prepared for the modeling convention: by videotaping myself.

I sang quietly into the webcam, so I wouldn't disturb Mom. When I played it back, it seemed to me I had been concentrating much too hard, maybe because I was looking at the words. So I did it again and again. Each time I finished recording, I told myself that it was going to be the last try for the night. But then when I'd play it back, I'd find more things I wanted to work on, such as breathing or eye contact. I always ended up doing another take.

Five hours later, I gave it a rest. By then, I knew the words by heart, and I still had several days left before the audition. I was tired, but knew I'd probably still end up waking up during the night, as had become my pattern. So I took a few more minutes to update my E-Me status: **Ashley is trying out for Camelot, and wishes good luck to everyone else who is doing the same!**

Then, I tried to sleep, but the music I'd practiced repeated over and over in my head, the way a buzzing mosquito torments you after dark.

I didn't realize it until I got to school the next morning, but the torment had only begun.

# CHAPTER 4

Someone had put a sticky note on my locker that read, *How will you get a part in the play if your stepmother doesn't pull any strings???*

It was clearly a jab about my modeling career, because Gabriella (my dad's girlfriend – *not* my stepmother!) had been the one who'd first suggested I consider modeling. But she had never pulled any strings for me, and I had actually signed with a big agency – not with Gabriella's small modeling school. With trembling hands, I pulled the note down and squashed it up. My first thought was that someone who had read my E-Me status must have written it. But then I realized that my name was on the audition sign-up sheet posted outside the drama room. Anyone could have known I was trying out, so there was no way to narrow it down. With the note still in my hand and indignant rebuttals whirling through my mind, I started down the hall to find a recycling bin.

Then it occurred to me that my rebuttals deserved a voice just as much as someone else's unfounded criticisms. Since the note wasn't addressed to me specifically, I decided to respond anonymously. I uncrumpled the note, and wrote underneath it: *The best way to get anything – good planning, hard work, and a big smile.* Then I took it down to the drama room and stuck it beside the sign-up sheet.

I jumped when I heard a voice behind me. "Hmm ... now I'm really confused," said a male voice I didn't recognize. When I turned around, I saw that it was Taiton.

Taiton was a senior. He had thick dark curls sticking out in crazy directions, eyes that changed shades from caramel to chocolate, coffee-colored skin, and a tall lithe body that almost never stopped moving.

Even when it looked like he wasn't doing anything, he was doing *something*. He doodled. He fidgeted. He tapped pencils and pens and played air guitar to songs only he could hear. He laughed louder and longer than anyone I'd ever met (which, if you knew my dad, was really saying something).

Everything that should have made him dorky somehow made him attractive. I didn't know him well, but I (like most girls at school) had always thought he was pretty hot. Now, I could feel his breath on my cheek as he leaned over my shoulder to examine the sticky note. His hair brushed against my ear, and I felt a shiver run down my back. Trying to speak in a normal tone, I asked what his confusion was about.

As he turned to face me, I couldn't help noticing his almost cat-like movements – quick, agile, and unpredictable.

"I'm confused about this," he said, reaching for the sticky note. I tried not to blush, but felt the heat rising to my forehead. "The dads I know aren't really big on their daughters doing nude modeling, so I can't see your stepmother getting you that kind of job. So, proposition: either it's not true that you relied on your stepmother to get you nude modeling jobs, which means this sticky note is absolute bull pucky," he said in a serious tone. "Or, proposition: the tales of you modeling naked are – sadly for us gentlemen – total fishlips." At this, he puckered up and did the best goldfish impression I'd ever seen. "Or, finally," he leaned against the door frame, "your stepmother *is* totally wicked, and she did get you unclothed modeling jobs. In which case, I would like to help you be free of her. But first, you'd have to show me the pictures."

A little cry of disbelief (or maybe horror) escaped my

lips as he crossed his arms and waited for my response. Absurdly, in the midst of his allegations of nude modeling, I recognized that his use of the word "proposition" had probably come from King Arthur's dialogue. I made a mental note to check the sign-up sheet afterward to see if he was trying out too.

I felt dizzy, but I didn't know whether it was because of his ridiculous claims or his ridiculously attractive grin. Hoping it was all really just some sort of bizarre flirtation, I mounted my defense: "Okay. First of all, there *is* a lovely woman dating my father, but she's not my stepmother. So anyone calling her that doesn't know the first thing about me." He tapped his fingers together and nodded rhythmically in agreement. "Secondly, the only nude pictures ever taken of me were bathtub shots when I was a baby. But if you didn't make up these rumors, I definitely need to know where you heard them." He nodded again, and I noticed that the halls had begun to fill up while we had been talking, so I lowered my voice. "And thirdly, if you're going to help me be free of anyone, you're going to have to assist me in figuring out who wrote the note." I ran my fingers up through my hair and exhaled in exasperation.

"All right," he smiled and put a reassuring hand on my shoulder, where it felt like it was going to burn right through my top. "I'll go back to my source and see what I can find out. And as for that note, I think someone else on that sign-up sheet probably wrote it, because they're worried about having some competition. I also think your response is right on. I wouldn't waste any more time worrying about it."

"Thanks," I said as the bell rang. "But I still feel kind of sick."

"I hope that's not my fault," he called out, walking away.

All through my morning classes, I struggled to concentrate. But my late nights had finally caught up to me. By lunchtime, I had a throbbing headache, but still no answers. Caitlyn and Conner didn't have any either.

"I did hear someone in the hallway joking about a girl posing nude," Conner admitted. "But it was like three days ago, and I didn't hear any names so I don't even know if it was about you, or something they saw online. Sorry."

"I haven't heard anything either," Caitlyn confirmed. "Are you sure Taiton wasn't just messing with you? I mean, you *are* single now – and it sounds like he was being kind of flirty. Maybe it was some kind of a twisted pickup line?"

"There's no question that he was trying to get a

reaction from me," I agreed, not admitting that it had worked. "But I didn't get the sense that it was just a move ... it seemed like he'd already heard something." I yawned and rested my head down wearily on my arms. "I wanted to work at the shelter tonight, but my head really hurts! I'm starting to think that maybe I hallucinated the whole Taiton thing."

"No way you hallucinated a hot guy like Taiton flirting with you," Caitlyn said, rolling her eyes at me. "You just need to get more sleep. I saw the time stamp on your E-Me post."

"Here," Conner said, handing me a Zoom Cola, "'twice the caffeine for twice the energy.' You look like you need this more than I do."

I took it gratefully. "It's not that I'm staying up too late," I explained, chugging it to try to force the caffeine into my bloodstream. "It's that I haven't been sleeping well the last week or so. I thought maybe if I went to bed later, I'd sleep more soundly. I could be getting a flu bug or something, though. Sleep plays an important part in maintaining a healthy immune system. I read that in my mom's patient information."

Caitlyn laughed. Turning toward Conner, she said, "Do you hear that? Your cola worked. Encyclopedia Ashley is back in business."

* * *

The following weekend, I found myself drinking another Zoom Cola at the fall fair. Cailtyn and I were celebrating her birthday.

"Are you sure you don't want some cotton candy?" Caitlyn asked for the third time, knowing it was one of my favorite treats.

"No thanks," I said. "I'm really enjoying this sweet liquid caffeine," I joked, taking another swig. I didn't admit that my mom's hair had started falling out that morning, and the idea of spun sugar wasn't sitting well with me.

She eyed me suspiciously. "You're not going to be, like, one of those Zoom Cola addicts, are you? I'm not going to return from Quebec to find you homeless, addicted, and begging for spare change?"

I laughed. "No! This is only my third one this week. Actually, it's only my third one *ever*. Plus, I've been telling my mom that it might be a good idea for her to start eating a more organic diet. I don't want to be a hypocrite, so this is kind of like my last hurrah."

"Come on," she said, grabbing my arm. "This is *our* last hurrah before I leave."

We checked out the exhibits – where Caitlyn had won some prizes for her artwork – and were making our way back through the midway when we noticed a trailer that said *Madame Syeira Sees All!*

"Hey! Check it out! Palm reading and Tarot cards! Let's get our fortunes told," Caitlyn suggested, grabbing my hand.

"I don't think so," I argued, shaking my head, surprised to hear my practical mother's voice coming out of my own mouth. "If Madame Syeira was the real thing, she'd have made her fortune from the lottery or something. She wouldn't be working here."

"You don't know that for sure," Caitlyn said patiently. "Maybe reading people is different from predicting stock markets."

At this point, she started going on about some famous artists who believed in the occult. I knew I should just go along with it because it would be fun, so I tried to play along.

She continued: "Besides, that sign says there's a discount if you get two readings."

"How about if I just pay for you," I offered. "Consider

it an early birthday gift."

"Nope. We're both going." She was determined, and I tried to justify the cost as entertainment. After all, it wasn't really any more wasteful than all the carnival games out in the midway. Reminding myself again that it was just for fun, I followed her in.

Inside, the trailer was dimly lit. I resisted the urge to point out how closely it resembled Professor Marvel's wagon in *The Wizard of Oz*, a movie we'd watched way too many times growing up.

"You'll need to come in one at a time," explained a woman in a sparkling robe and dangling bracelets.

"Why do we have to come in alone?" I asked, suspicious that if she was working a scam, maybe it included rifling through our purses when our eyes were closed.

"So your energies don't get mixed up," she smiled and blinked at us through her fake eyelashes. "It gives a clearer reading." I couldn't quite figure out her accent and questioned whether it was even real.

"I'll go first," Caitlyn said. Just to be safe, I grabbed her purse as she stepped through the beaded curtain.

Five minutes later, Caitlyn emerged with a large grin. Her fair skin was slightly flushed, and I could tell by the breathless way she spoke that she'd heard good things.

"Your turn," she urged me forward. "And then I'll tell you what she said about me."

I was still looking around suspiciously as I sat down, and because I wasn't paying attention, my watch caught on the tablecloth. The Tarot cards, which had been stacked in front of me, flew off the table and fluttered down around my feet.

"Oh my gosh – I'm sorry!" I said, embarrassed by my klutziness and bending down to collect the cards. It was kind of like a twisted game of 52 Pickup – not that I knew how many cards there were in a Tarot deck. But at least, I was relieved to see she didn't have wires or hidden cameras under the table.

"No, no! It's okay," she said, motioning for me to stop. "Come, sit down. If the cards fall down, it means they aren't right for you. I'll read your palm instead."

I sat down and held my hand out to her. Her hands were warm, as if she had a fever, and as soon as she began tracing my palm with her fingers, it seemed as if the heat from her body was rushing into mine. Suddenly, my hand started shaking, my heart began to race, and I felt dizzy. I yanked my hand out of her grasp, and looked around to collect my things.

"I don't think a palm reading will work for me,

either," I explained over my shoulder.

"No refunds. But, here. At least take this." Madame Syeira closed my palm around a ring.

"I think she just felt me tense up," I said later, to Caitlyn, when she asked why I hadn't gone through with it. But really, I'd just wanted to get out of there. "She knew I thought it was all bogus, so she made up some non-sense about blocked energy fields rather than admit it," I explained.

"I thought she was pretty good," Caitlyn said, after I had settled down. "She knew I was taking a trip."

Caitlyn had made notes about her reading while I'd been inside, and she spent a long time going over them with me, trying to find hidden meanings. To me, everything the woman had said was so vague it could apply to anyone. For instance, she told Caitlin she saw "lots of tears." Caitlyn thought this referred to her ex-boyfriend, but *everyone* has tears in their lives. Happy tears *and* sad ones. Like my mom. Still, Caitlyn seemed beyond pleased with her fortune.

"Here – try this on," I said, handing her the ring Madame Syeira had given me instead of the reading. "She said it would help unblock my energies, but I'm not feeling it. Let's see if it does anything for you."

I handed Caitlyn the black ring.

"Check it out!" she said, moments after putting it on. "It's changing color!"

Sure enough, the dark, inky stone was shifting to a bright, turquoise blue. I knew it just had something to do with body temperature, but Caitlyn, after checking the accompanying color chart, declared that black meant I'd been "stressed and tense," whereas she was "calm and relaxed."

"You should keep it," I told her in all seriousness. "Because if my mother thinks I'm stressed, she'll feel guilty, and that will cause *her* more stress, which she doesn't need."

"If you're sure," Caitlyn said. "But why wouldn't she think it's reasonable for both of you to be just naturally stressed out right now? With everything that's going on, I mean. It's not like you can just decide you're not going to let the cancer bother you."

I agreed. "But there are things you can do to reduce stress, like yoga and meditation." I checked Caitlyn's face to see if she thought I'd gone crazy mentioning meditation. But she just looked interested, which was one of the things I loved about her. She was as nonjudgmental as I was skeptical.

"How can they do that?" she asked, twirling the ring around her finger.

"Well, a lot of the stuff I'm reading says that excess stress causes your body to release too much of a stress hormone – cortisol, I think – and that messes with your immune system and makes you more prone to disease. So if you meditate or do yoga, it can get rid of some of that stress."

"I don't want to dismiss anything that you think might help," Caitlyn said softly. "But when it comes to your mom, your stress theory sounds kind of like blaming the victim. I thought cancer was mostly just random – you know, except for smokers and stuff."

"You mean that if stress caused it, then it's kind of like my mom's fault, because she wasn't dealing with the stress properly?"

"Yeah," she said, shaking her head. "I don't think that's fair. It's like when I thought that if I were a better girlfriend, Tyler would treat me better. But *I* didn't cause his anger issues. And I don't think your mom's stress caused her cancer."

"Maybe not. But it can't have helped. And she needs to consider every possibility these days. That's why I'm trying to get her to eat more vegetables."

"Then you need onion rings," Caitlyn declared, springing to her feet. "They're all vegetable!"

Caitlyn and I had such a good time at the fair that day that I almost regretted talking her into going away. But her ring was still bright turquoise as she waved good-bye from the bus that Monday morning, so I knew she felt she was doing the right thing. I waved until I couldn't see the bus anymore. Then I looked down at my own bare hand, wondering what color the mood ring might be if I had kept it to wear to my *Camelot* audition that afternoon.

# CHAPTER 5

I didn't know many of the people at the tryouts in the gymnasium. There were several younger girls I'd seen in the halls, a few seniors, and two girls from my class, Amanda and Destiny. As much as I was beginning to appreciate the story of *Camelot,* I was kind of wishing that Mrs. Emrich had chosen a musical with more female parts. There seemed to be far more girls than guys at the audition, and the girls would probably all want the part of the queen. Fleetingly, I wondered whether any of them had written the nasty note I'd found on my locker.

On the other hand, there didn't seem to be very many guys trying out, even though there were so many roles for them. And, as Conner had quipped, they were going to get to play-fight with toy swords, practically every boy's dream.

I did know Amanda and Destiny, but not well. Both of them had been in *Oliver* the year before, and the word around school was that Destiny was quite serious about becoming a professional actress.

I was just deciding where to sit when Taiton came in. The sign-up sheet had been removed long before I'd remembered to look for his name on it, and I hadn't run into him in the halls since that day when he'd told me about the rumor.

I worked my way toward him, struck once again by the warmth of his smile.

"Just the girl I wanted to see," he said. "I have news!" He started air drumming, and I wondered how, if he got a part, he would ever be able to stand still long enough to deliver his lines.

A tightness began forming in my jaw, and I knew I wouldn't be able to sing well if I was thinking about the rumors. "Later, okay? After my song?"

"Okay," he said, hitting what I imagined was the cymbal on his imaginary drum set, then motioning toward the chair beside him. I took the seat just as the auditions began, and breathed in his scent. We couldn't really talk aloud anymore because of the people on stage, but he whispered that he wasn't trying out for either Arthur or Lancelot, despite evoking Arthur's signature "proposition" line during our first meeting.

"King Pellinore," he mouthed, whipping his hand around as if brandishing a sword. I recalled that Pellinore was King Arthur's old friend. It was a non-singing part, but the character was a bit of a clown, always chasing after some monster. It seemed like a great choice for a guy so comfortable in his own skin.

Even though other students had started trying out already, it felt as if *we* were the ones being watched as we sat in the audience. Maybe it was because we were both new to the Drama Club, and most of the others were returnees. Or maybe it was just the combination: tall, hot senior reputed to "play the field" sitting with brunette just out of a long-term relationship. Or maybe nobody was actually looking at us, and it was me who was judging, comparing, wondering how I could be so interested in this quirky guy who was so different from my first love.

I stood when my name was called. Taiton reached out to pull a tiny piece of lint off my sweater before telling me to "break a leg." It was nothing, really, but somehow it felt intimate, and it unnerved me to think that just a moment before, I'd been imagining what it might be like to kiss him.

Although the spectators had remained fairly quiet during the other performances, the silence seemed deeper when my turn came to sing. Trying to harness the spotlight to my advantage, I stood up straight, tossed my hair back, and made eye contact with the audience as if walking a runway or doing a photo shoot.

But just before the music began, the football team loped into the gymnasium. They were dressed in full gear, apparently on their way to the locker room. Mrs. Emrich glared and held up her hand to stop them in their place.

It took only a fraction of a second for me to spot Brandon among his teammates. I'd watched enough of his games to know him by the way he moved – chin up and a small bounce to his step – without even seeing his number. He stared when he saw me, clearly surprised that I was on a stage. But, looking back at him, I thought I saw pride there too, and maybe a flicker of nostalgia for our time together. And there it was. I was unexpectedly caught in a surge of emotion. It started in my belly and churned through my body. It felt like a mix of love, hurt, fondness, and broken dreams, a feeling so intense that I hadn't allowed myself to admit it since that night he had ended our relationship up on the hill.

Fortunately for me, it was exactly the right emotion I needed to deliver Guinevere's words about trying to forget a love she couldn't have, and to make the song my own. I found myself looking directly into Brandon's eyes as I began with the opening lines of "Before I Gaze at You Again."

The music spoke of needing to cry and grieve, before moving on from one you've loved and lost. Though I felt every word like pinpricks in my heart, I kept my voice strong by pulling my eyes away from Brandon and directing my gaze toward the rest of the audience.

When I finished, the crowd applauded with an energy far more powerful than anything I'd experienced as a model. I trembled with the realization that I had pulled it off. Bowing slightly, I smiled in gratitude. But when I looked for Brandon, I realized the football team had left.

Taiton was just finishing his own audition an hour later when my cell phone vibrated. I was surprised to see that Brandon had sent me a text.

> Can u meet me on the hill, now?

The hill behind the school was where I used to watch his football games, and where we always had our important talks. It was there that we'd broken up, and there where we'd reconnected as friends just weeks earlier.

>> Sure, I replied.

He was already waiting for me, stretched out, pulling up blades of grass and flinging them into the wind.

"Hey," I said sheepishly, embarrassed by the emotions

I'd expressed onstage, though he couldn't have known he inspired them. "How's your semester going?" I asked.

"Okay. Strange. A couple of guys asked me if they could take you out. *That* was weird." He shook his head, staring down at the grass.

"Anyone cute?" I asked, not intending to make him jealous, but trying to be funny instead by reminding him that, in the beginning, *he* was the one who had wanted to "take a break" and "see other people."

I saw his whole body relax as he tossed his head backward with a snort of laughter. "None as cute as me," he retorted in the same spirit. Then his eyes met mine. "And nobody good enough for you."

"That's sweet," I said.

He smiled. "You were really great up there."

"Thanks ..." I turned my face toward the goal posts and pressed my lips together to avoid saying anything I might regret.

"How's your mom doing?"

I debated about how much to say to him, but Brandon and I had been through so much during our two years together that I figured I could count on him to be cool about it. "She's tired a lot. Her hair is starting to fall out, which must be hard on her. But we don't really talk about it. She's rooting for me to get a part in the musical, which kind of gives her a chance to play 'stage mother' behind the scenes. Mostly, it sucks. But we're managing."

"Good," he said. "That's all I wanted, actually. Just to tell you that you were phenomenal, and to make sure you were okay. I know it must also have sucked to drop out of the exchange."

I didn't need anyone's pity, least of all Brandon's, and suddenly wished I hadn't been so brutally honest with him. I'd been plucking grass from the lawn while we spoke, and had collected a pretty good handful of it before dumping it back on the ground. "I'm trying new things anyway," I said, wiping the grass off my pants as easily as I brushed away his concern.

I went straight home, knowing I shouldn't have been angry with Brandon, but feeling as if he'd somehow taken something away from me again. I was still trying to figure it out when I walked into the house and found Mom sitting in the kitchen.

She handed me an electric razor.

"You – want me to do your hair," I said, stating the obvious, but not knowing what else to say. I started shaking all over.

"Not 'do' it. 'Remove' it," she said unemotionally.

"Because?"

"Because another big chunk of it fell out into my hand this morning when I tried to brush it. And I can't stand to lose little bits of myself, piece by piece," she said, her voice getting smaller as she pulled out a clump of hair for emphasis. "I just want it to be over."

My mom didn't do bad hair days. She had naturally thick, dark hair like mine, which she always kept perfectly styled. She never had to resort to elastics or clips like most other women. It wasn't that she was vain or conceited. She just believed in doing her best at *everything,* including personal grooming. The idea of her being bald was – to me – unimaginable.

I understood that her request wasn't so much about her hair as it was about her need for control. If she cut her hair, then she wouldn't have to feel like the cancer was taking it from her, the way it was already taking her health and her dignity. But still.

"Maybe if I just trim it a bit?"

"No," her voice was firmer now, resolved. "All of it off. Now."

My hands shook almost as much as the electric razor as I drew the clipper over the first swath of hair. It slid down her back onto the floor, leaving behind a scruff of short hair I'd have to brush off once the clipper had handled the longer strands.

I worked in silence, not even telling her about Taiton, or Brandon, or my audition. It was all I could do not to cry as clump after clump fell at my feet. I was glad she couldn't see my face. She hated pitying looks even more than I did.

Without her hair, she looked small and vulnerable. But when she spoke, I could hear that my mom – my demanding, powerful mother – was still in there.

"Okay," she said, as if we'd just finished the dishes. "That's done, then."

"It'll probably grow back thicker," I offered. "And maybe with curls. By this time next year, you could have a whole new look."

She smiled at me, with a quivering expression that I didn't realize until later had nothing to do with curls. "Let's hope so."

And it wasn't until later still, after Mom had already been dozing for hours, and after I'd sent Caitlyn a lengthy e-mail about the day, that I decided to just try a few of the all-natural sleep aids I'd purchased for my mom.

In just one day, I'd made it through Caitlyn's departure, my audition, a heart-to-heart with my ex-boyfriend, and shaving off my beautiful mother's hair. I had too many things whirling around in my brain to let go and sleep. As I shut down my computer – the sleep capsules had already started to kick in – I remembered that I had never had a chance to hear the news Taiton wanted to share.

# CHAPTER 6

The next morning, I woke up early but feeling rested and refreshed – it had been so long since I'd really slept soundly that it felt like I'd slept in for hours. I dressed, did my hair and makeup, and still had time to offer Mom some breakfast before she headed out to the hospital for another round of chemo.

"Nothing for me today, thanks," she said, grimacing. Sliding a hand over her smooth head, she added: "I don't know how it's going to go ..."

"You'll take the NausGone with you, right?" I urged. "They seemed to help last time."

"We'll see," she said. "The oncologist said she was going to put me on a different anti-nausea drug. Maybe I'll do better with it."

"Hopefully," I said, kissing her on the cheek. "I know you haven't had much of an appetite lately. I've been thinking that maybe, since you're eating so little, we should try to make that little bit that you do eat count."

She looked at me, puzzled.

"I'm thinking about trying some different recipes – some organic ingredients, more vegetable protein. Easier for your body to process," I said.

"Oh – don't worry about that right now, Ashley," she smiled. "People have been so generous about dropping off food, and your father's always trying to buy me ice cream at the hospital – though I think that might just be an excuse for him to try the new flavors. We have to trust the process. When my body really needs food, I'll get my appetite back."

"Okay," I said, realizing that a chemo day probably wouldn't be ideal for trying ratatouille and lentil pie, but hoping I could still talk her into it another time. "I'll skip the shelter after school, and get home as soon as I can," I assured her.

"I'm going to be here whenever you get home – don't rush," she said. "The animals need you too." For a moment, I studied her bald head and thin frame, torn between feeling proud of the way she was coping and angry with her for not acknowledging that I was trying to be supportive.

"Wait," she called, as I headed out the door. "I forgot

to ask you – how did your audition go?"

"Really well," I told her, pleased that she'd remembered. "I don't know if I got the part, but I gave it my best shot."

"That's all you can ever do," she said. "I'm proud of you."

Taiton was leaning against my locker when I arrived, tapping out a beat with his hands by his sides.

"I drove you away last night with my acting?" he asked. I winced, remembering that Brandon's text message had arrived during Taiton's audition.

"No ... sorry, I just got a message, and had to take care of something," I explained, embarrassed that I'd left so suddenly, but flattered that he'd noticed.

"No big deal," he said. His shrug was genuine and perfect. It wasn't a fake I'm-going-to-pretend-I-don't-care-so-I-can-look-cool shrug, nor was it an I-so-can't-be-bothered-with-you gesture. It was just an honest, whatever-you-want-to-do-is-okay-with-me shrug.

"If I had your cell number or you were on E-Me, I could have let you know," I added, feeling bold, even a little flirtatious.

"I don't need any of that stuff," he said, playing with the buttons on my jacket sleeve. "Who needs to be in touch 24/7?"

I felt a little disappointed. If he didn't want me to be in touch, he couldn't have been that upset about me leaving without saying good-bye.

"So," I began, reluctant to start in on him right away about his "news." "What brings you to my locker?"

He glanced across the hall and said, "Wait a sec – I see someone *we* need to talk to." When Taiton came back, Cory was with him, and I could see by the way Cory shook his head that they were having a disagreement.

"I'm telling you, I didn't make it up," Cory told him. "She mentioned it to me and Allie on the first day of school. Ask her if you don't believe me."

Thinking back to that first day, I recalled Cory asking for my autograph. But I couldn't imagine what he was referring to. "Ask me what?"

"You told us that you quit modeling because you were asked to pose naked, no?" he said.

I swear, if I'd had a drink in my hand, I would have thrown it into the air the way cartoon characters do when they're surprised. "What? NO! Where would you get that idea?"

He looked confused.

"You said you were uncomfortable with what they wanted you to do. Allie and I figured that meant naked pictures or something. You know, because you're such a goody-good."

His voice seemed very far away as he spoke, and suddenly I didn't seem to have enough air in my lungs. I slid down my locker onto the floor and gazed past the two of them at the ceiling.

I was vaguely aware that Cory and even Taiton, who seemed to me was always in perpetual motion, stood frozen, looking down at me while I digested Cory's words.

I wasn't a goody-good. Brandon and I had done stuff. Not everything. But lots of stuff. Not that it was anyone's business.

Maybe I should have called Cory an idiot or something, or pointed out the absurdity of his assumption, but as soon as I caught my breath, the whole thing became hilarious. I couldn't stop laughing. Soon, I was laughing so hard that I got the hiccups, and that made me laugh even harder.

Stunned at first, Taiton and Cory started laughing too.

"That is so far off base, I can't even tell you," I finally said. "It was fur – not skin! They wanted me to model animal fur, but I just couldn't stomach it."

"Ohhhhh," he said. "That makes so much more sense. You didn't tell us exactly what happened though, so we just assumed."

Regaining my composure, I stood up and looked him right in the eye. "I didn't go into the details because I know wearing fur is still a touchy subject for some people. I didn't want to have to debate my side of it all year."

"I'm really sorry," he said, looking sheepish. "Our theory seemed to make sense at the time. We weren't totally sure, though, because some people say you're a goody-good, and other people say you and Brandon were together so long that you must have ... you know."

"We're talking about modeling, right?" I redirected him. "So can you just please do me a huge favor and explain what really happened to anyone you shared your theory with?"

"Yeah, I can do that," he agreed. "Sorry again."

"Mystery solved," Taiton said as Cory walked away.

"Thanks," I said, watching his eyelashes flutter.

"So what excuse am I going to use the next time I want to talk to you?" he asked, brushing back the hair from my eyes.

"How about the one where my best friends just went to Quebec without me, and I'm not sure who to eat lunch with?" I offered, surprised at my boldness.

"That'll work," he said.

* * *

Later that night, I e-mailed Caitlyn. I knew the goal of the exchange program was language immersion, but I needed to check in with her. Caitlyn and the other participants were supposed to be speaking French all the time. They were advised to limit English to once or twice a week. I didn't know when she'd be able to read my message or when I'd hear back from her, but I wanted to fill her in on what was happening here. I told her the basics, trying to emphasize that things were okay even though I missed her.

* * *

Taiton and I started eating lunch together all the time. Although I wasn't exactly sure what it meant, I began to look forward to spending my time with him. He never asked questions about anything unless I brought it up first. When I talked, he listened attentively, and often had interesting ideas. Case in point: on the first day that we ate together, we talked a bit more about modeling.

"The thing was," I told him, "I wanted to try it, and I wanted to be the best I could at it. But I was never entirely comfortable being judged solely on my looks."

"You mean like the way King Arthur sits around before his arranged marriage to Guinevere, worrying about whether or not she'll be beautiful?" Taiton replied. "I find that part of the musical kind of strange, considering what a forward-thinking guy Arthur turns out to be. They're supposed to spend their whole lives together, and he doesn't ask whether she's intelligent, kind, witty, or anything."

I didn't say it, but when he talked about stuff like that, I found Taiton to be pretty "forward-thinking" himself. And I wondered why such a liberated guy would have such a reputation as a player.

"You're totally right," I agreed. "But it's not like he could send her a text message to find out if she was smart."

"No," he said, stroking his chin thoughtfully. "But he could have asked her to lunch."

And while lunches at school quickly became something I looked forward to, dinners at home were proving more challenging.

Mom's second chemo treatment made her sicker than the first, despite her new meds. Every evening, after stopping at the animal shelter – where at least I felt like I was being helpful – I continued trying to coax Mom into eating healthier foods. But no matter what I offered her, she just wasn't interested.

By Saturday, I was desperate for Dad's advice on how to get through to her.

As always, Daphne greeted me at the door. Even though she always stayed with my dad, we had a great bond, and she never had any trouble transitioning between the two of us. In some ways, it was kind of like our own joint custody arrangement. Her delight in seeing me made me feel even guiltier about how little time I'd had to spend with her.

Before I'd even taken off my jacket, she flopped over for belly rubs. After, she brought me a squeaky toy to toss around. As we played in the living room, Dad and Gabriella asked how things were going.

Although Dad and I had spoken to each other almost every day over the past few weeks, we had very few conversations that didn't revolve around Mom. Now, a few weeks into the school year, Dad seemed to remember that I did have other – though perhaps less important – things going on.

"So how's the semester going?" he asked.

"Not too bad," I admitted, thinking for what might have been the millionth time how fortunate that was, considering my sleep issues and busy schedule. "I set up my timetable with easier subjects this semester because of Quebec ..."

"Oh, that's right!" Gabriella sympathized. "You were going away – I forgot!"

"But I've tried out for *Camelot* at school. We should hear about casting next week," I explained. "If I get a part, I'll be a little busier."

"In addition to all your worries about your mother ..."

"Mom was a lot better this week. Tired, but that's a completely normal side effect of the chemo," I explained.

"Ashley got her some natural anti-nausea stuff that really seems to work better than what they give her at the hospital," Dad explained to Gabriella. "Which is great. Just don't bring home any of those funny brownies people are always talking about." I didn't think his cheesy humor was very funny, especially when he started laughing at his own lame joke.

Gabriella apparently didn't see the humor in it either. She told Dad she knew of a few people who had done really well with alternative cancer therapies. I considered whether it might be worthwhile having her talk to my mom about them, because I wasn't getting very far with her myself.

Apart from running her modeling school, Gabriella managed the Looking Good/Looking Up program at the hospital. The program helped cancer patients feel better by pampering them with beauty treatments. Kind of like the smile-and-your-body-will-release-feel-good-chemicals theory. That was where Dad had first met Gabriella, when he'd taken Mom in for a doctor's appointment. Gabriella met a lot of different cancer patients there. So it made sense that she might have some insight into the usefulness of alternative therapies.

"Do you know anything about diet?" I asked. "My big concern right now is that she's not eating very much, and when she does eat, it's mostly junky comfort foods," I said, shuddering at the memory of the night before, when she'd said she couldn't stomach anything but pudding or Jell-O. Her eating habits had never been unhealthy before, so it was strange to see her gravitating toward sugary snacks now. "I'd like her to try some organic things, to avoid putting even more chemicals into her body, and help strengthen her immunity."

Gabriella shook her head. "I don't know a lot about it, but I think you're right to provide her with healthier options." Then she reached out to take my hand. "And you know you can call me anytime, if you need to talk, okay?"

As much as I appreciated her offer, I was relieved when she went home early, leaving Dad and me to eat alone. It was good to have him all to myself again.

Over dinner, I opened up to him a little bit more about some of the things I'd been trying to tempt Mom with, like simple stews with beans and legumes for protein. Ever since the first chemo session, even the idea of meat nauseated her.

"Ashley, I don't want you to think you have to take care of her all the time. And your mom feels the same way. This is not your responsibility. Knowing you're there if she needs you is all your mom needs. Are you sure that you're okay?"

"I'm fine. I'm just not sleeping well, but that could be a growth spurt or something. And I'm not just trying out the new menus because of Mom's illness. I've been wanting to change our diet for a long time. It could be good cancer prevention for me someday if I start now."

"Good thinking," he said thoughtfully. "But *Camelot*'s going to be one heck of a show if you get a part and the beans you're eating make you gassy!" he said, shamelessly laughing at his own joke again.

# CHAPTER 7

On the day that Mrs. Emrich read the cast list over morning announcements, I barely heard her, being half asleep from going to bed too late and getting up too early again. I'd always helped out around the house, but now I'd taken over all of the laundry, food preparation, and cleanup. Plus, I still had my volunteering at the shelter and homework. I didn't mind doing it. In fact, I actually liked playing house, and feeling like a part of my mom's recovery process. But I still wasn't sleeping well unless I used sleep aids.

So while I heard Mrs. Emrich say my name, I didn't hear which part I'd gotten. It was Allie, sitting across the aisle, who turned in her seat and said, "Oh my gosh! Ashley! You got it! You got Guinevere!"

I looked around, stunned, as if I'd just woken up, and saw that other people were smiling at me, and nodding their heads. I was happy, but I don't think I smiled as much as I would have expected. I guess it didn't feel real because I hadn't heard it myself. I quietly sat there trying to process what it meant.

It wasn't until I heard someone behind me mutter, "Well, I hope she doesn't quit partway through because she doesn't like the wardrobe." Shaking, I turned around, but I wasn't even certain if it had been a male or a female voice. Nobody behind me gave any indication that they had a problem with me. Still, the bitter words flattened any excitement I might've been feeling.

It was almost more humiliating to be thought of as a quitter than as a nude model. At least those rumors were ridiculous enough that most people (I hoped) would have dismissed them. The "quitter" accusations, on the other hand, must have stemmed from jealousy. I considered making a loud, retaliatory comment like, "No way am I going to quit such an amazing part," just so the mumbler would know I'd heard them. But then I didn't want to make it seem like I was gloating, or rubbing it in by responding. Plus, even though I didn't have any siblings, I'd spent enough time around Brandon's family to know that attention-seekers usually stopped if you ignored them. Too bad I couldn't respond anonymously, as I had with the note on my locker.

Taiton, who'd also landed the part he'd tried out for, seemed to agree with me. "People who won't say stuff to your face aren't worth confronting," he observed.

That afternoon, I did check carefully to see if there was anybody else from my homeroom who might have wanted my part. While Shelby and Chris had both auditioned, they hadn't tried out for singing roles. Destiny and Amanda, on the other hand, had both tried out for Guinevere, so I approached them with cautious congratulations.

To my relief, they both smiled warmly at me, praising my good fortune.

"Congrats, Ashley. You'll make a really good Guinevere," Destiny said.

"Thanks," I said, sitting down beside them. "Either one of you would have been great in the part. You gave me some tough competition."

Amanda exhaled loudly and then said, "Yeah – a lot of people expected Destiny to get it, but I've been telling them that the male leads really carry this play. And Guinevere is supposed to be very beautiful, so I suppose it makes sense to let you try it – even if we don't know yet how well you can act."

I'd been getting used to the anonymous digs at my modeling. But I stood there wondering if I'd heard her correctly. It was the kind of insult that knocks you off balance, because it comes buried in a compliment. I knew I couldn't really do it, but I wanted to swat her like a mosquito that had drawn blood. Based on the warm smile with which she'd greeted me with and the coolness of her remark, I decided that Amanda must be a pretty good actress herself.

"Why wouldn't you think I can carry the role?" I asked her.

"Didn't your mother get you your modeling job or something? We just figured this was more of the same."

"No," I said icily. "I planned well, worked hard, smiled genuinely and got a contract from a prestigious agency all by myself," I said, flashing my bright smile for added effect. It wasn't like me to brag, but I was a hard worker, and I resented the implication that I hadn't earned the modeling job or the part of Guinevere. And I hoped she'd caught the reference to my sticky-note reply, because it seemed very clear to me that she had likely been the one who'd written it in the first place.

"What's your problem?" Amanda asked. "You aren't even a model anymore anyway."

"No, but I *am* Guinevere," I replied, walking away. I hoped she hadn't seen the way I was shaking.

"Do you think I was too awful to them?" I asked Taiton later, as he walked me out of the building.

"Definitely not," he assured me. "King Arthur was the nicest guy around, but he still said Queen Guinevere and his best friend Sir Lancelot should be punished when they betrayed him." He deepened his voice and spoke in a kingly tone as he repeated some lines from the story.

"How do you do that?" I asked. "We just got the scripts, and this is the third time you've quoted the play to me."

"Can you keep a secret?" he grinned. "I love musicals. And I've been watching *Camelot* on DVD since I was a little kid."

"That's so great!" I laughed. "You don't do cell phones or e-mail but you watch musical theater? I never would have pegged you that way – even after you tried out."

"Why not?"

"I don't know. I guess I was buying into the stereotype about guys who like musicals," I admitted, staring at the floor.

"A lot of people do," he said. "So don't out me, okay? I've got a reputation to maintain." He touched the tip of my nose with his finger.

"You mean, you don't think Destiny and Amanda

would understand?"

"I doubt it. But I have to say, you demonstrated a lot of restraint back there."

"I don't know," I said. "I was *really* pissed, but I was trying to play it cool. Sometimes I think it would be more satisfying to just let my emotions all hang out. Maybe self-control is overrated."

"Maybe it is," he said, taking me by the hand.

* * *

With the cast assigned, rehearsals were scheduled for three nights a week – two devoted to acting and one to our songs. We were all going to be spending a *lot* of time together.

Destiny and Amanda seemed to back off after the first day, and most of the others were very supportive. Destiny didn't even seem jealous that her boyfriend, Ryan, was playing opposite me as King Arthur.

"You know what the one problem with this story is?" Ryan asked one night, after we'd read lines together.

"You tell me," I said.

"No kissing scenes," he replied. "My girlfriend talked me into doing this. And now that you're my stage wife instead of her, we have the perfect cover to fool around a bit."

As much as I wasn't into Ryan, and I wouldn't have dreamed of upsetting his relationship with Destiny, I also didn't want to appear to be a goody-good. "It really is too bad, since you were the only reason I tried out," I said theatrically.

Taiton appeared behind me at that moment, and I hoped he hadn't heard me joking around with Ryan. But even if he had, I knew he would be cool. We hadn't formalized our relationship in any way, and apart from some occasional hand-holding, there wasn't any traditional boyfriend/girlfriend stuff going on.

The one thing that *had* changed was that ever since the night he'd first taken my hand, he had incorporated me into his endless fidgeting. Instead of drumming beats on tabletops, he often played with my hair, or traced the outline of my face.

My mom, who'd always been very cool about guys, quietly cheered me on from home. She asked all sorts of questions about Taiton. They seemed to distract her from feeling so crappy. I found myself trying to identify new things about him just so I could share them with her.

When she felt up to it, she also helped me practice my

lines. And because of all the time we were spending together, in some ways, I was feeling closer to her than ever.

But we were still clashing over her health.

After Gabriella had affirmed my idea of at least giving alternative therapies a chance, I'd returned to the natural food store where I'd first bought the NausGone.

The store was called Naturally Good. It had old wooden floors that creaked when you walked on them, and smelled comfortingly of nuts, flour, and yeast. They sold bulk goods out of large see-through bins with big metal scoops.

I went in looking for just a couple of items for my mom: organic fruit for smoothies and shark cartilage pills.

Even though I'd researched the things I was looking for, a tiny part of me wondered whether they might make people laugh some day. I mean, up until the late nineteenth century, people believed that draining people's blood would cure them of illness. But bleeding actually killed a lot of people instead. None of the things I was searching for were drastic in that way. But still.

Part of me also suspected that radiation and chemotherapy might also one day be viewed as useless and barbaric. The treatments made everyone feel so much worse before they got better. But I also knew that for now, they were the best we had, and statistics did seem to suggest that they helped. Still, it made sense to me that my mom should replenish her body with vitamins and minerals while she was doing the chemo. I just had to convince her of it too.

I'd just found the shark cartilage when the clerk came by and glanced in my basket. "Are you shopping for a cancer patient?" she asked me gently.

I nodded, surprised that I couldn't find any words, and then managed to say, "My mother's doing chemo for breast cancer."

She smiled, and I noticed that she was naturally very pretty, even without makeup. "The shark cartilage is a great idea. We cater to a lot of patients in similar situations," she said. "And I can recommend a couple of other things that might prove helpful."

Her nametag said "Harley." I had a hard time believing a woman with such a tough sounding name could be so soft-spoken. It reminded me of the animal shelter, where people sometimes brought in Great Danes named "Tiny" or Teacup Yorkies named "Killer."

Whatever her name, she seemed very knowledgeable, and I found myself listening intently. She talked about some of the holistic treatments I'd read about, and a few other treatments I hadn't, like vitamin and mineral regimes to replace the nutrients displaced by the chemo. And the way she explained things about cancer and immunity – it all seemed to make so much sense. I couldn't see how my mom could possibly balk at any of it.

For instance, she recommended an energy supplement she suggested would be excellent to revitalize and renew energy.

"And not just for people with cancer," she explained. "I take it all the time. Much better than coffee or energy drinks. And no sugar or chemicals."

"Really? I did try your sleep aids a few times," I acknowledged. "I bought them for my mom, but she's so exhausted that sleep is never a problem. I don't think it ever would have occurred to me to buy real sleeping pills at a drugstore, but these have been great."

"Oh, I agree. And I think you'd find that the energy supplements, our Rev-Its, really work too. It's all about balancing your inner energies, you know? There's a lot of stress and toxins in our environment that throw our systems out of whack. If you're a busy student, I bet you'd love the energizers. And if you face a lot of stress, you should also consider these Calm-Its. They're kind of like natural Prozac, but they don't make you lose your appetite."

"My mom won't admit to being stressed," I told her,

"but I'm sure she is."

Mom was my first priority so I checked all of the labels carefully to make sure that it would be okay for her to take everything together. None of the products I'd picked up said anything about avoiding other medications or alcohol (not that that was going to be a problem) or operating heavy equipment, the way regular cough and cold medicine always did. They also didn't have any of the scary warnings about other conditions that I usually found on over-the-counter drugs – like *"Do not take if you have heart, liver, kidney, or thyroid conditions."*

But when I got home, Mom wanted nothing to do with them.

"Ashley, what is this for?" she sniffed, holding out the bottle of shark cartilage I'd handed her.

"Cancer prevention – or cure, depending on what you need," I said. "Sharks don't get cancer."

"But sweetie, no matter what your father may have told you about our divorce, I am not a shark." It was exactly the kind of joke I would have expected Dad to make, but it surprised me to hear her say it.

"I know," I hugged her. "But some people think sharks have special immunity or something, and that you can get those immunities through their cartilage."

She looked skeptical, but I kept pushing. "Just try it – it won't harm you." When she didn't protest further, I opened the bottle. The room was immediately flooded by a dead fish stench, so strong that we might as well have been in the dumpster at the back of a seafood restaurant.

The cat seemed interested, but Mom, thoroughly nauseated, made a mad dash for the toilet. I cursed myself for not having opened the bottle beforehand. Now I'd never get her to try it.

Food was still a problem too. She couldn't even stomach a smoothie. "Everything tastes garlicky and metallic all the time, even my saliva," she complained as she put a piece of chewing gum into her mouth. I hated to see her so miserable, but it *was* funny to watch my prim and proper mother stuff her mouth with giant wads of spearmint gum.

# CHAPTER 8

Caitlyn sent a couple of text messages telling me that her exchange partner, Mireille, was – as expected – wonderful. She then congratulated me on getting the part in the play.

I got a more detailed update via e-mail, which I accessed from my dad's laptop while over at his place.

> I wanted to call you to tell you this because it is HUGE, but I couldn't wait. I'm not supposed to be using English, though, so I have to make it quick. I'm at school now and don't want to get caught! We had this school dance thing on Saturday, and Conner told me he wants to be more than "just friends." (Did you just squeal a little bit when you read that? I'm betting you did.) So I'm freaking out here! I like him, but I didn't know for sure that he liked me that

**way (I know you said he did, but I seriously didn't believe it). Now that I do, I'm scared of it not working out and ruining our friendship. I wish I could talk to Mireille about it, but we still have a total language barrier. I can't coherently explain all the stuff that happened between Tyler and me, which is another reason why I'M FREAKING OUT. Anyway, Conner said he doesn't mind waiting a bit while I figure it out. He even said he'd always be my friend no matter what, but STILL! OMG. I wish you were here!!!**

She was right about the squealing; I *was* freaking out too. Daphne had been on the couch beside me, lying contentedly on her back with all four legs up in the air as I'd turned the computer on. I actually jumped out of my seat, almost knocking her off, when I read Caitlyn's news. She sat up, startled, and wagged her tail at me as I screamed out "Oh my gosh" over and over. Then I went back and reread it out loud as if Daphne could understand the e-mail.

Tyler had been Caitlyn's first boyfriend, and he'd turned out to be a total jerk – manipulating her into stuff she wasn't ready for and actually getting physically abusive. But Conner, on the other hand, had never been anything but respectful toward Caitlyn. They'd both been kind of crushing on each other for a while. I was thrilled that he had finally made a move – even if it *was* going to mean more inside jokes between them. But I also understood her hesitation, in light of how things had turned out with Tyler, who had at first seemed like every girl's dream come true.

I knew I needed to write my response to Caitlyn carefully, especially since I'd totally blown it with her when she'd first started dating Tyler. Early on in their relationship, I was kind of shocked to hear how far the two of them were going – physically – when they'd been dating for a lot less time than Brandon and me. Later, I realized that Brandon and I were only thirteen when we started dating, so things had progressed more slowly between us. On the other hand, Caitlyn and Tyler got together two years later, when they were already fifteen and sixteen. I hadn't considered those facts when I first expressed my surprise to Caitlyn, and she'd shut me out because I was being judgmental.

I adored Conner, and thought he was perfect for her, so I wanted to say the right things this time:

**You're right – I am freaking out here too! But in a good way, because I think it's about time, and I am SO happy for you! Please don't feel like I am pushing you into anything you aren't ready for, but I think you should go for it. Even though you're worried that it might mess up your friendship if things don't work out romantically, you have to remember that the friendship has already changed because he put his feelings on the line.**

Even as I wrote the words to Caitlyn, I knew I wasn't ready to take my own advice. Taiton was gorgeous, and when he was near me, sometimes it was all I could do not to touch his hair or his skin. Because I was missing Caitlyn and Brandon, my friendship with Taiton had come to mean a lot to me. I wasn't willing to risk the changes that would follow a romantic move on my part. But Conner had already taken that risk with Caitlyn, and I wanted her to embrace it. I continued to write:

**I know you regret a lot of things that happened with Tyler, but remember that**

**your mom found a really good guy after your dad left. I think that's proof that you can learn from your mistakes and make better choices (even if my own mom is still looking for Mr. Right). Conner's ideal for you. It might sound dumb, but I've always thought that the way he puts other people first with little things, like holding the door open or saying "thank you," kind of shows that he is considerate by nature. That counts for A LOT in a relationship. Plus, he's kind to animals :). So as long as you're CERTAIN that his electric-blue hair comes out of a bottle, and not a bad gene pool (in case you want to have kids with him some day in the distant, distant future ...), you should go for it. Thanks for sharing this amazing news with me, even at the risk of getting caught by the English Police!!! I wish I could be there with you.**

As I finished the e-mail, I started thinking about Brandon and how he had also been a great choice until he decided we should see other people. Up until that moment, I had really believed I could be one of those girls who marries her high school sweetheart and lives happily ever after. But if we hadn't broken up, I might've never had the chance to know some of the other fascinating (and hot) guys I'd met since then. I decided I needed to tell Caitlyn something else I'd been considering in light of my mom's illness:

> **Also, regrets aren't always about the things you tried that didn't work out. Sometimes they are about having been afraid to try something that might have worked out beautifully.**

After I hit send, I started to think about my own regrets. Very few were over things I'd actually done. Most fell into the second category – things I should have done but didn't. Like, I should have been less judgmental with Caitlyn about her relationship, so she would have confided in me when things began to go wrong. I would *always* regret that. Then there were the opportunities I'd missed because I thought they'd always be there waiting for me – like going all the way with Brandon, which I'd just figured would happen when the time was right. Now, it never would. Then again, I knew that if I had rushed it, I might have regretted not waiting, because it was still likely that there were other great loves ahead of me (even if Madame Syeira hadn't predicted it for me).

I was still thinking about regretting things I'd never done, and was seriously considering calling Taiton, when my phone rang. Unwittingly, I bought into Caitlyn's psychic beliefs for just a fraction of a second, thinking it might be him. But when I looked at the number, I saw that it was my mom.

"Can you ask your father to come in for a few minutes when he drops you off tonight?" she asked. "I want to go over a couple of things with the two of you."

* * *

"So you seriously have no idea what Mom wants to talk to us about?" I asked Dad again as he pulled into the driveway. The last time we'd had a family conference, it was to let me know that the surgery and radiation hadn't worked and that Mom was about to start chemotherapy. I think I could be forgiven for being a little paranoid about another big group discussion.

"No idea. Honest," he said, turning off the ignition.

Then he grinned and added, "Unless she's trying to pawn off your bean dishes on me!"

Mom was waiting for us in the dining room. She had a lot of papers spread out around her, but I don't think Dad noticed them at first because he still wasn't used to her bald head. Her eyelashes had also fallen out. Even I was still startled sometimes by the dramatic change in her appearance, so although Dad had already seen it, I understood why he caught his breath before composing himself.

"Nice to see you without your head in the toilet!" he said, trying to be funny.

"It'll probably be back there on Monday when I start the next round of treatments," she teased back. "But at least this way," she smiled and stroked her bald head for emphasis, "I won't have to worry about getting my hair caught in the whirlpool when I flush!"

It was exactly the kind of toilet humor my dad was famous for. But usually, my mom hated stuff like that. I watched in horror as the two of them laughed at the "joke" my formerly dignified mother had made at her own expense.

"That's not funny!" I whined, noticing how the blue veins in my mom's scalp throbbed with the rhythm of her laughter. "And if you'd just try some of the other things I keep recommending, maybe you won't be as sick this time," I added, annoyed that she was still resisting some of the natural remedies I thought she should try.

"Oh, sweetie," Mom said, wiping tears from her eyes. "What can we do except laugh about it?"

"Umm, you could try absolutely everything possible to boost your immunity?" I said, as I sat down at the table.

"You know, laughter is actually one of the proven immune system strengtheners," Dad said. "And it doesn't mean we aren't taking your mother's illness seriously just because we can find a giggle in it now and then."

I thought back to the moment when Taiton, Cory, and I had laughed together at the whole "nude photo" misunderstanding, and how I'd felt so much better afterward. I knew Dad was right. But I just didn't think there was anything funny about cancer. I took a deep breath and stared at the wall across the room.

"Are you okay, honey?" Mom asked, looking into my face with sudden intensity.

"Just tired," I said, trying to steer clear of the emotional charge I felt building up in the room.

"Well, I just have a couple of things I'd like to talk about with you and your dad, but I promise it won't take long," she said. Despite her serious tone, I felt my body relax at the familiarity of her approach.

"This," she continued, indicating the papers in front of her, "is a new copy of my will, and some Power of Attorney documents." My stomach clenched at her words, and I actually had to concentrate to hear what came next. She was all business as she spoke. "I've been meaning to do it for a while, but today was the first day I really felt well enough to do it. The will is completely standard, and Ashley, as a minor, of course you know that if anything were to happen to me, your dad would automatically take over full guardianship of you. That hasn't changed – I've just updated it to add in some more specifics about your college fund," she said, handing it over to my dad.

I tried to concentrate on what she was saying. "What *has* changed is the power of attorney," she turned and addressed me directly. "That's the document that gives someone else the ability to make medical and financial decisions on my behalf, should I become incapacitated. I realized the other day that I hadn't changed it since Rob and I were married." Rob was the second (and briefest) of my mom's three marriages.

I sat in stunned silence as she continued talking about the possibility of her own infirmity. Still speaking directly to me, she said: "So, since my family is out of town, I think it makes sense for your father to take over in this capacity. I know he'll always have your best interests at heart, so he really is the best person to take charge if there *are* difficult decisions to make."

My dad nodded, and tried to make another joke. "Yeah, I'm pretty much over the bitterness from our divorce. So you can probably trust me not to pull the plug prematurely," he winked at her, and she doubled over laughing *again*.

Both of them stopped when I stood up. "Why is all of this so funny to you? And why are we even having this conversation? Cancer sucks, okay? It sucks that you had to have surgery and radiation and now you've lost your hair. It sucks that you're probably going to spend the whole next week puking all over again, and those things ARE NOT FUNNY! But maybe, if you'd quit putting all of your faith in your doctors and whatever fate has in store for you, and actually try a couple of the extra things I've researched, you won't die. I just don't see why we need to talk about wills and decisions and ... and ... plug pulling!"

I had never yelled at either one of them, and the looks on their faces told me they were even more surprised by my outburst than I was. Shaking, I shoved my chair away and stomped off before they could stop me. I heard my mom's protests behind me. "Nobody is saying I'm going to die, Ashley. But I need to be responsible and prepared, just in case!"

She must have been trying to follow me, because my dad cut her off and said, "Let her go. This is hard on her," as I slammed my bedroom door shut behind me.

# CHAPTER 9

I flung myself onto my bed and lay there feeling miserable about what had just happened. It made sense that my mom felt like she needed to get her stuff in order, especially since she was a total planner. But she didn't need to act like she was dying when she hadn't even tried everything that was available to her. And she shouldn't have *joked* about it in front of me. It wasn't as if she had a lot of money or property to leave, or as if I would someday be fighting it out with a bunch of siblings. It was just me. Alone.

Normally, when I was upset, I'd go to Caitlyn's. That's where I went right after Brandon and I had broken up. She'd talked me through it and listened while I ranted, asking all the right questions so that even though it still hurt, I felt better.

Caitlyn and I had been best friends since sixth grade. Once Brandon and I started going out, though, I'd barely made any time for Caitlyn (something I will regret forever).

I'd thought that romantic relationships took effort, but that my friends would always be there for me. Now, I realized I should have tried to balance my social life. Although I had other friends, *she* was the one I shared the important stuff with, like my mom's illness. That kind of openness didn't come easily to me.

Still, I wasn't sure whether I needed to talk to someone about the problem, or just find a way to get over it alone. I was mad at my parents, but I was even angrier with myself. My mom was out in the dining room writing a will in case she died, while my dad joked about it. All my life, she'd told me to do my best, but as far as I was concerned, she wasn't doing her best to beat her disease. For example, I'd given her actual studies showing that meditation could release endorphins, but she hadn't even considered it seriously. After less than five minutes listening to the meditation CD I'd purchased for her, she declared that it just wasn't her thing. Apparently, she felt ridiculous picturing a mountain inside her body, though, to me, a mountain was better than a tumor on any day. After that, I knew there was no way I could get her to try visualization exercises where she was supposed to picture her white blood cells attacking the cancer cells. Those didn't have as much scientific backing, but I didn't see how they could hurt.

Stress could hurt her recovery, and since she wasn't going to reduce it by meditating, I needed to act more maturely and not freak out like a little kid. It was hard not to be upset, though, when I was under so much stress myself. Then, I remembered the Calm-Its I'd purchased at Naturally Good. It sounded as if Mom and Dad had moved out of the dining room and into the basement, so I headed into the kitchen for a few capsules of "all-natural relief from anxiety and nervousness."

An hour later, Dad called up to me: "Goodnight, Ashley. Don't forget to come out and feed your cat before she has your mother for dinner!"

A bit later, Mom knocked on the door to say she was going to bed. "Honey? I know you're still upset, so I'm going to let you be. I just wanted you to know that I'm here if you need me."

I didn't reply, though the Calm-Its had definitely helped. I wasn't as angry anymore, and I was starting to see that Mom was just trying to look out for me, the same as she'd always done. But I did still think she should have warned me somehow. I wasn't ready to leave my room yet, never mind apologize for my hissy fit. Instead, I finished my homework and updated my E-Me page by paraphrasing a quote in the musical: **Being alive is ever so much better than being dead.** I knew the wording wasn't exact, but after a night of cancer drama, it captured exactly the way I was feeling. Then, I surfed the Internet for video uploads from the *Camelot* performances at other high schools. As if he knew something was wrong, Taiton phoned.

"Hey," he said. "How are you?"

I knew better than to disclose everything, so I kept it simple: "Better – now that you've called. What's up?"

"Well," he said, and I could hear music thumping behind him, "now that we have our scripts, and you know my little secret, I was wondering if there's any chance you'd want to watch the *Camelot* DVD with me sometime?"

It only took me seconds to reply.

"Ummm ... what about now? Would that work?"

Even when Brandon and I had been dating for a long time, I rarely had him over so late on a school night. So even though it wasn't really a big deal, I felt kind of reckless setting up a movie date with Mom already asleep.

Still, I did need to learn how to deliver our lines. I also knew I probably wouldn't be able to go to sleep without a couple of sleep aids anyway. Better to use my time constructively than to lie awake all night, or to waste the evening on E-Me.

"Now could work," Taiton answered in his deep voice. "Your place or mine?"

Up until then, our relationship, if you could call it one, had been strictly school-based. I hoped I wasn't playing the game wrong by being so direct. I'd never been to his house, and he'd never been to mine. I glanced at the clock and saw that it was already nine. By my calculations, it would be well past one in the morning if I had to ride my bike over to his place, watch the movie, and get home. But he had a car.

"My place," I said. I gave him directions, and then went to fix my makeup.

Taiton arrived within twenty minutes, movie and snacks in hand. As always, he smelled like clean soap, and I wondered whether he'd stopped to shower before coming by. He probably would have if he'd considered it a date. I hadn't actually been sure when I asked him over whether I wanted anything other than a friend to hang with. But when he bowed down on one knee and called me "M'Lady" – as he would do in the musical – I felt a jolt of electricity race down from the nape of my neck to the top of my jeans.

I led him downstairs to the biggest television Mom owned (which, by Dad's standards, was still kind of like a baby television). Taiton explained to me that we were about to watch the film version of the stage production, as opposed to the movie version. I only half-listened, distracted by how his dark hands moved so expressively when they didn't have something to fidget with.

By the time the opening credits were done, his hands weren't empty anymore – they were holding mine.

Having him over was exactly what I'd needed. I wasn't thinking about time commitments, cancer, or anything except the way our hands fit together. I wondered if I could ever sing as beautifully as the Guinevere we were watching. We'd read through the whole script during rehearsals, so I already knew that my character was caught in a love triangle between her husband, King Arthur, and his best friend, Sir Lancelot. I'd seen some of the clips on the Internet too.

While Taiton's long dark lashes distracted me, I also got a lot out of watching the story with Taiton pointing out small details.

"Watch here," he'd say, bouncing his knee up and down in excitement. "See how Guinevere kneels down to Lancelot? She's not supposed to do that, because she's the queen, and he's beneath her in status."

"How come you've never done the musicals at school before?" I asked, suddenly recognizing a love of theater on his face.

He shrugged. "Watching them and being in them are two different things."

"So why now?"

"Because it's *Camelot*!" he grinned. "And for my school transcripts. I do okay, but I'm not as academically-inclined as you. So I try to look well-rounded with a broad range of extracurricular activities."

"Okay – one more question?" I asked.

"You can ask fifty if you want," he replied, tracing a giant number five in the air while making a zero with his right hand.

"How'd you get so into musicals?" I asked.

"They helped me learn English. Musicals and *Sesame Street*. I was five when we moved here, and I didn't know the language. I learned my letters and numbers on *Sesame Street*. Then someone told my mom that most people lose their accents when they sing, so she started buying us musicals to sing along with and improve our pronunciation."

"That's so cool," I said. "Is she excited about you being in the show?"

"Not really," he shook his head, and tapped out a rhythm on his thighs. "My mom and dad say they came here so I'd have more opportunities, and they'd rather I focus on schoolwork – extracurricular activities be damned."

"My mom used to be all about me doing my best at everything," I said, surprising myself with my honesty, but not wanting to stop once I'd started. "But now that she's got breast cancer, she keeps saying I'm only going to be young once, so I should get out there and have fun."

"Lucky for you," he said, touching the tip of my nose with his finger.

I waited, wondering whether he'd try to take things any further than hand-holding. I'd heard that he'd gone out with a lot of other girls in the past, so I wondered what might be holding him back with me. But the anticipation was so sweet, that I didn't dare spoil it by asking.

It was almost two in the morning by the time Taiton left. I tried getting ready for bed, but if anything, it seemed like I was more awake than ever. Not wanting to lie awake all night, I took two of the sleep aids and fell into a heavy slumber.

When I finally awoke, I discovered that it was nearly noon. I'd slept in sometimes when I was staying at my dad's, but I couldn't ever remember sleeping all morning. And my mother had certainly never let me sleep in on a school day.

"You were awfully tired," she said warily, as I came

downstairs. When I didn't snap back at her, she continued: "So I thought I'd better let you sleep."

"Thanks."

"You're not coming down with anything, are you?"

"I don't think so ..." I said, yawning, feeling like I'd wasted half my day. "I'm really sorry about last night." I brushed the hair out of my eyes and took a couple of steps toward her.

"It's okay," she said, hugging me. "It's a hard thing to talk about, at any age, but especially at sixteen."

I nodded, glad that she understood.

"So why so tired?" she asked, running her hand through my hair.

"I ended up inviting Taiton over to watch *Camelot*."

She raised her eyebrows with interest. "And ...?"

"And it went longer than I expected," I finished.

"Hmm," she creased her forehead, which, without hair, made her look a bit like a *Star Trek* character. "You don't have to go to school this afternoon if you don't want to, you know."

Mom offering to let me stay home for no reason was even more unexpected than her letting me sleep in. Part of me wanted to accept, just to see what she had in mind, but I shook my head. "I can't afford to get behind in school work or they'll kick me out of the musical. Plus, I have rehearsal until four-thirty, and then I promised to stop by the shelter." I checked her face for signs of disappointment, and then offered: "But I can skip the shelter if you need me home sooner."

"No, it's okay," she said. "I think it's great that you're still involved in so many things. But after that big sleep you just had, I was worried that you might be overdoing it."

"I'm fine," I promised, kissing her on the cheek. But as I showered and dressed, and the fog in my head failed to clear, I realized I'd been mistaken. So I took a couple of Rev-Its and bought a Zoom Cola on my way to school.

# CHAPTER 10

I didn't know whether it was the Zoom Cola, the Rev-Its, or maybe just the extra sleep, but I felt so energized that afternoon that I had to be reminded several times to recite my lines more slowly. I also cleaned the shelter's litter boxes in record time, and, when I got home, I peeled and pitted four kinds of fruit to make a smoothie for my mom.

"This is good," she said after tasting it. "No beans."

I didn't tell her about the almond milk I'd added – or the organic eggs – because she didn't really need to know. But I was beyond happy that I'd finally come up with something nutritious, protein-packed, and tasty for her.

I tidied up, practiced singing, and finished my homework before getting to bed. It was a busy day, but with the help of the herbal supplements, I felt both rested and energized. I was hoping my mother would notice my condition and ask for some herself.

"You're acting awfully happy today. Is Taiton putting

you in this good mood?" she asked with a big smile.

Taiton had asked me out for Saturday night, and Mom was reading a lot into it. "It's a bonfire out at the beach," he'd explained. "Probably the last one before it gets really cold. It sounds like a lot of the cast is going. And you've been so busy lately, you really ought to get out and experience the simple joys of maidenhood," he said, referring to one of Guinevere's songs.

Though we saw each other everyday, we hadn't met outside of school since our movie night. I hadn't asked him why that was. He knew I was busy, and maybe he was trying to be respectful of that.

* * *

Mom was up reading when I got home on Friday after school. I'd suggested several times that she should try journaling about her cancer experience, but she hadn't taken my advice. I still felt selfish doing fun things while she was stuck at home.

"Of course you should go!" she said, smiling, when I suggested staying home from the party. "When you're sixteen, Friday nights should be about hanging out with your friends."

"I just wondered if maybe you'd want some company or something," I said, still feeling guilty.

"No – you should go. I'll probably just end up back in bed soon anyway. I've already told you – I don't want you to spend the whole year staying in with me and then regretting it later."

It made me happy that Mom wanted me to have a healthy social life. Part of me really wanted to go, but it had been a long week and I was tired. Almost reluctantly, I hauled myself out from under the cat and off the couch. I made Mom's smoothie, but I skipped dinner, telling her I'd probably get something on the way. The truth was that I just didn't feel like making anything for myself, or having to clean it up afterward.

I knew I was going to need some extra energy to stay out, so I double-checked the Rev-Its bottle to see if I could take more than the ones I'd had earlier. The label said only "take as needed to restore energy," and "do not exceed eight caplets in twenty-four hours, except under the advice of a physician." I took a couple of tablets before getting ready to go out, and I popped a few more in my pocket for backup.

Taiton was driving, and I'd hoped to be ready when he arrived, but all the hesitating on the couch had put me behind schedule. I was still up in the bathroom when I heard the bell. Mom answered the door. As I came down the stairs, I could see from Taiton's face that he was just as laidback with my mom as he had been with me. It was one thing to have the door answered by someone in a bathrobe and curlers, but quite another thing to be greeted by a bald woman in baggy pajama pants. Still, he appeared completely unfazed and I felt my shoulders loosen up as I realized that Mom (who had always been concerned about appearances) didn't seem to be at all uncomfortable.

"My gosh, your mom is pretty," Taiton said, when we were in the car. "Even without hair. You look a lot like her."

I don't know if that was the moment that the Rev-Its finally kicked in, or if it was just the thrill of receiving a sincere compliment from a guy I genuinely liked, but suddenly, I was ready to go out and have a great time. For myself and for my mom, so I could tell her about it later.

We made a quick stop at the convenience store on the way out of town, to pick up snacks: Zoom Cola, flavored popcorn, and black licorice.

"Why do you drink that stuff?" Taiton asked, motioning his chin toward the cola.

"Sometimes I'm just really low on energy," I admitted. "And it tastes better than coffee."

He shuddered mockingly. "I can't handle all that caffeine. Makes me jumpy," and I laughed at the thought of him being any jumpier than he already was.

Most of the cast was already at the party, along with a lot of other people from school. Some kids had brought guitars, but they were competing with car stereos and the waves, so it was hard to hear them. At first, we just mingled and talked to other people, but then all of a sudden, time seemed to speed up. Before I knew it, I was laughing and dancing and telling jokes. Someone had a camera, and someone else asked me to pretend I was on a professional modeling gig. So I posed in the most ridiculous ways possible. *Everything* was funny that night – from the way I kept falling down in the soft sand to the way Ryan – the guy who was playing King Arthur – leaned in and ate half a stick of licorice right out of my mouth. Just after he'd told me that black licorice is known to increase blood flow to certain important areas of the body.

"Is that *true*?" I'd shrieked, loudly enough for several people to look up questioningly before I doubled over laughing again.

"Absolutely," he assured me. "And as your 'husband,' I can prove it to you, if you'd like."

"That has to be, like, the cheesiest line ever," I giggled,

hoping I wasn't hurting his feelings. And hoping, too – even though he was just kidding – that his girlfriend, Destiny, hadn't heard him.

"Come on," Taiton whispered in my ear, taking my hand. Then, he wrapped his arm around my waist, and pulled me down onto his lap. His breath smelled delicious, like hot chocolate and mints, and his crazy hair was even wilder in the wind. We weren't doing anything more than talking and holding hands – albeit with me in his lap – when Ryan came over holding my bag of popcorn, and dumped it over our heads. That, too, struck me as hilarious as we shook it off our hair, and I found myself reaching down to pick it out of my bra.

"You were different tonight," Taiton said, kissing my forehead as he dropped me off. "It was nice to see you out, really having fun."

"I just felt really *good* for the first time in a long time," I said. "Maybe it was you."

He smiled and traced the outline of my lips with his index finger. "No, it was you – you had this energy around you tonight."

As he spoke, I looked down and realized that not only was my heart racing, but my hands were shaking. I held them behind my back, hoping he wouldn't notice. I realized that my body was in overdrive, and my brain was on high alert. The dashboard lights of his car seemed excruciatingly bright, and the engine now seemed to roar in my ears.

After I'd thanked him for getting me out of the house, I tiptoed in as quietly as I could and went upstairs. I brushed my teeth, changed into pajamas, and took some sleep aids, as had become my routine before going to sleep. It had been an especially fun night, and I felt so much more comfortable with the other cast members. Yet for reasons I didn't understand, I found myself crying alone after I'd gone to bed.

My phone woke me up the next morning. I assumed, by how sleepy I still felt, that it must be early Saturday morning. But a quick glance at the clock by my bed told me I'd slept past eleven again.

"Ashley?" Caitlyn's voice said on the other end of the line.

"Oh my gosh – hi! It's so great to hear from you!" I said, sitting up in bed.

"Well," she said, "I've been wanting to talk to you all week, and this morning I realized I *had* to."

"How come?" I was waking up, but still held the phone away from my mouth so she wouldn't hear me yawning.

"Well, I take it from the pictures on E-Me that things

are getting serious with your hunky co-star!"

"What pictures?"

"Allie posted them," she said. "You haven't seen them yet?"

"No – what are they?"

"The album says 'Beach Party,'" she said. "And there's a picture of you in Taiton's lap, so you'd better dish."

I couldn't believe that Caitlyn was so far away and had already seen what I was doing the night before. I took a couple of minutes to fill her in on what (little) had been going on with Taiton and me, and then asked her about her own love life.

"I'll get to that later," she said. "But in the meantime, you'll never guess what else has happened." She was right – I couldn't imagine what might have happened that could be more important than Conner.

"My father sent me a birthday card," she said. "My *birth father*. It went to my mom's, and she forwarded it here. He wants to have contact with me now."

Caitlyn hadn't seen her biological father since she was four. And she hadn't really known him before that, either. I thought she'd be excited to meet him. But as she talked, she explained that she'd discovered he'd been convicted of a DUI and some other serious charges. She felt like that was a good reason not to become involved with him.

While she was *saying* she didn't want to hear from him, I recognized a slight hesitation in her voice, and some uncertainty beneath her bravado. Being careful not to just tell her what to do, I tried to suggest that she give it some more thought. "What if something happened to him, though, and it was too late to change your mind?" I asked gently. "Like, what if he ... got cancer or something?"

"What if *I'd* had cancer during all those years I never heard from him?" she asked indignantly.

"That's not the point." I knew it was up to her, and that maybe she'd just called to talk, not to get unsolicited advice from me. But I'd been thinking a lot about what it would mean to not have my mom around, and I didn't want her to miss out on the chance to have a relationship with the father she'd never known. "The point is, he's trying to reach out now. Maybe you should consider giving him a chance while you still have the opportunity to get to know him."

"You've always had both of your parents," she said. "You don't understand what it's like to be abandoned by one of them." I know she didn't mean to be hurtful, but even though both of my parents had been around for my entire life, it wasn't as if I had two parents raising me under one roof. Still, I tried to think of something I could say that might be helpful.

"What about talking to him to find out about your genetics?" I asked, still thinking about my mom's cancer. "It could be really important to know your family history."

"That doesn't seem like such a good idea, now that I know there could be alcoholism in my family tree," she said ruefully. "Anyway, I've got to go."

Later on, I was still considering gentle ways to advise her as I logged into my E-Me account. It turned out that she'd beaten me to it and sent me a personal message:

> Thanks for listening this morning. Sorry I didn't really get a chance to ask you about your mom or tell you more about Conner or Mireille, but I have been using way too much English lately. Anyway, except for the thing with my dad, things are mostly good here and I was glad to hear that they are going well for you too. Hope your mom is okay. Sorry if I seemed grumpy.
>
> Love, Caitlyn

Having first read Caitlyn's message, I hadn't yet seen

the party pictures she'd referred to earlier. But then I saw that Allie had tagged me in quite a few of them, and a couple of other people had posted their photos as well. When I'd been modeling, I'd been constantly surprised by how makeup and lighting could change my appearance in a photo, but now I was amazed at how my energy level could change it. The girl that Allie had tagged as me was *not* the groggy girl I was that morning. The girl in the pictures had no reservations and no worries. She was sixteen, and living it up. And she definitely didn't look like a goody-good.

In one of the fake "modeling" shots, you could see my hand on Taiton's chest, and my back leg kicked up in a flirtatious manner. At someone's suggestion, I'd stuck my tongue out as if I was licking him just to make it extra cheesy. Caitlyn – referring to my modeling days – had written **I can't believe you used to charge people for what you're doing here for free!**

Part of me couldn't believe I'd acted so brazenly the night before. When I remembered Cory's comments about the nude modeling, I hoped he – and other people – wouldn't read too much into them. On the other hand, at least people wouldn't think I was a total goody-good anymore. Still, I smiled when I saw Caitlyn's comment, thinking about how supportive she'd always been of the modeling. So many of the other girls I'd met in the industry (and now, back at school) had been jealous and petty. Then I added my own comment beneath hers: **But when I do it for free, I'm free to use my tongue! LOL.**

Another picture had been taken right after the popcorn incident. In it, I had popcorn all over my hair, my lap, and the ground around me. The guys sitting near us also had it on them, as they'd begun a food fight shortly after it had been dumped. Caitlyn, referring to the mess I'd made, had written: **Could you spread it around any more?** It must have seemed funny to her to see me in the middle of a mess like that, knowing how much of a neatnik I'd always been. Looking around at my room, though, with last night's clothes still scattered around where I'd dropped them, it was clear that orderliness had taken a backseat to my other interests and responsibilities.

By the time I'd logged off and made it down to the kitchen, Mom was waiting to hear about the party and Caitlyn's phone call. I filled her in, enjoying the chance to relive the fun I'd had, but still stifling yawns even though it was almost noon.

"Taiton seemed very nice," she said when I'd finished, "But you guys are going to have to start coming in earlier if you're going to be this tired all the time!"

"I know," I croaked, trying to clear out a tickle in my throat.

By evening, the tickle had become a full-blown sore throat. When I logged back onto E-Me before bed, I discovered that the once-funny comments had taken on a really nasty tone.

Quite a few people had seen the pictures and posted their own comments about them. And apparently, nobody was still thinking of me as a goody-good. Under the picture where Caitlyn had commented about me posing for free, a guy from Brandon's football team had put: **Free goes with EASY, right?** Another guy had written: **If you'll do it for free, does that mean I don't even have to buy you dinner?** And some person I wasn't even friends with wrote: **Feel free to use your tongue on me ANYTIME.**

The comments people had added under the popcorn photo were similar to the others. Clearly, people were misinterpreting the comment about "spreading it around" to mean that I was a slut, which hurt, because it was completely unfounded.

For a few minutes, I sat there, staring stupidly, not knowing what to do. Then I started feeling sick, and wanted to cry.

Based on how Cory and Allie had misunderstood my modeling story earlier in the month, I guess I shouldn't have been surprised that the pictures and the comments had taken such an ugly turn, but still, I was astonished by how many people had responded. Worst of all, I'd played a big role in it, by posing so stupidly and commenting back to Caitlyn the way I had. I just hadn't clued in that anyone else would care so much, or be so gross about it.

My chest felt tight and my throat burned as I tried to talk myself through it. *It's just some stupid comments,* I thought to myself as I wiped away tears. *Nothing serious. Not like cancer. Not like chemotherapy. Not like having a sick parent. This stuff doesn't matter,* I tried to convince myself. Not fooled, I bit my cheek until I tasted blood.

# CHAPTER 11

When I got over the initial shock of finding myself ridiculed by what seemed like the entire world, I e-mailed Allie, asking her to take them off her page.

**Oh my gosh, I am such an IDIOT!** she wrote back. **I didn't think you'd be upset because you and Caitlyn were the first ones to comment.**

Obviously, I *also* hadn't realized that I would start something so upsetting. I mean, people commented about pictures and status posts all the time. It was part of what made E-Me so appealing – the immediacy of being able to share your thoughts, or make a joke. And although I *had* been kind of suggestive when I'd made that stupid comment about using my tongue, I really hadn't expected so many people to notice, let alone care. I hoped removing the pictures would delete them from people's minds.

**Sorry to be such a wuss**, I wrote back to Allie. Then, trying to blame my discomfort on extenuating circumstances, I added: **It's just all getting kind of gross, and I wouldn't want Brandon to get the wrong idea about how I've moved on.**

Then, thinking it might still be best to tackle the issue head-on, I updated my E-Me status: **Ashley is ... sorry.**

By Monday morning, my sore throat had progressed into a raging head cold and turned me into a hacking, snorting, phlegm factory. I hadn't had a cold that bad in years, and there was no way, between coughing, snuffling, and blowing my nose, that I could have focused on school. Plus, I would have infected everyone within twenty feet of me, so I asked my dad to pick me up and take me to his house for the day.

Mom only had another week before her next chemo treatment. I knew her immunity was probably low from the previous rounds, and I didn't want to risk giving her my cold, which could delay her next treatment cycle.

"Ooh – you look like you should be in bed," Dad said as I climbed into his car, wads of tissue in hand.

"I know," I said, dabbing gently at my inflamed nose. "Mom needs my company right now, but I really don't want to add this to her miseries."

"Well, it's really very selfless of you to share your germs with me," he teased. "And you know Daphne and I miss having you stay over. But I want to remind you again that it is not up to you to look after your mother."

Despite his words, I still felt guilty as Mom waved – bald-headed and frail – from the door. Knowing something and believing it are two very different things.

"I know," I sniffed again. "But still ..."

"I know," he parroted back to me, nodding. "But your mom's a tough woman, and I'll make sure she's okay. You've probably let your hectic schedule run you down, Queen Guinevere."

"I have been pretty busy," I admitted, "But I thought I'd be okay. I've been taking vitamins and everything."

"You'll be okay," he said, putting his hand on my shoulder. And for a moment, I considered telling him that I was also kind of relieved to have an excuse to stay home from school until the rumors and jokes died down. But he would have wanted specifics. Under normal circumstances, I might have considered telling Mom. But it was way too embarrassing to share with my dad. I figured I'd taken care of it anyway.

At Dad's, I slept – without the sleep aids – all that day, and the next. It almost seemed funny when Dad popped in at Mom's house a couple of times and reported back to me that she was, indeed, functioning, because I clearly wasn't.

By Wednesday, I still wasn't completely recovered, and I didn't think I'd have much of a singing voice. But I wanted to get back to school anyway, before I got even further behind in my classes and rehearsals.

Bolstered by a cup of strong coffee, a couple of herbal energizers, and some over-the-counter decongestants, I made my grand return. Alas, the E-Me "jokes" from the weekend hadn't been forgotten as I'd hoped.

Someone had stuck a note in my locker. They'd printed off the photo of me with my tongue sticking out, and had written across it: *U can lick me anytime.* A phone number was scrawled across the bottom.

The coffee I'd had for breakfast threatened to erupt from my belly like an angry volcano as I stared at the number I knew I would never, ever want to dial. I grabbed a hold of my locker door as a second wave of nausea surged through me.

"What's wrong?" asked a voice I'd know anywhere. I looked up to see Brandon beside me, peering over my shoulder.

Quickly, he snatched the note from me before I realized what he was doing.

He pressed his lips together for a second, and I saw his forehead crease just a bit. "So *that's* what the guys were talking about in the locker room last night."

Everything around me felt like it was moving fast, and kind of tilting sideways. "What do you mean?" I asked.

He shrugged, as if to show me he didn't care, but I could hear in his voice that he did. "Someone said you were doing some private modeling the other night."

"We were just goofing around."

"They also said you were high or something."

I shook my head, feeling my eyes watering up at the thought that Brandon would believe a lie like that. "I was just having a good time. I was out with a friend, and I was in a good mood. That's all it was. You know I don't do that stuff."

"That's what I told them," he reassured me. "I know you. But you seem ... different. Are you okay?" His tone was neutral, but his eyes were searching mine. "Is Taiton treating you all right?"

"Sure. He hasn't broken my heart yet," I snapped, angry that people were spreading lies about me, but taking it out on him. Then, seeing the hurt on his face, I softened.

"Look – I'm sorry," I said. "I just ... I have a cold, and I don't really know where I stand with Taiton – which is too weird to talk to you about. And there's still a lot going on at home. And now this crap is on the Internet and on my locker. Not to mention that you're looking at me like I'm an injured dog who might bite you. I didn't mean to be so crabby."

"It's okay," he said, pulling me in for a hug. "It's just some stupid gossip. I was just worried about you."

Taiton's attitude was similar to Brandon's. "Keep your cool," he counseled, "and this will blow over too."

By the end of the day, I'd begun to think that Brandon was right. Nobody in any of my classes had mentioned anything about the E-Me posts, and I realized that the note had probably been sitting in my locker for a couple of days already, while I'd been off sick. It seemed – for a few hours – that things had blown over after all.

Rehearsal was another story. Despite the medications, my voice was still hoarse and Mrs. Emrich kept telling me to speak up.

"Or lick it up," I heard someone whisper behind me. I turned, glaring as I straightened my shoulders, but no one gave anything away. I didn't have any problem confronting people who were being jerks – to me, or to anyone else. But I wasn't going to start a public spectacle without knowing who had made the remark. And there was no way I was going to go whining to a teacher about it, because I didn't want to give the idiot attention-seekers that kind of satisfaction.

Taiton threw me a look that said he'd heard it too, and I saw him take a step backward so that he was behind the others. I wasn't sure whether it was so he could watch them for me, or just because he was constantly in motion.

I fumbled through my next couple of lines, until Mrs. Emrich called a time-out.

"What's going on?" she demanded, though not unkindly.

I explained that I had been sick, and was still just a little woozy from the cold medicine.

"Okay – why don't you head out and get better?" she offered. "We can work on some of the other scenes tonight."

"Thanks," I said, grateful not only that I could rest, but also to be getting away from what felt like icy stares from my cast.

After thanking Mrs. Emrich, I flashed my best I-can-totally-take-it smile at the others. Back at my locker, I loaded up my backpack with all of the schoolwork I'd missed during my absence, and left with the best of intentions.

But the thing was, even though I left rehearsal early, skipped volunteering at the shelter, and went to Dad's house instead of Mom's, I never actually did any homework that night.

I let Daphne run around outside while I used my laptop to check E-Me, which, thankfully, contained no new surprises. Still, I didn't trust it to stay that way. I worried that people might have made copies of the pictures, and that they could resurface at any moment. I worried that whoever had whispered at rehearsal was going to get louder, and more confrontational. And I was mentally berating myself for not being able to just let it all go when most of the school seemed to have moved on.

Taiton called after rehearsal to check up on me.

"I'm looking for Kickass Ashley," he teased. "You know – the one who doesn't let crude comments get to her?"

"Knew her once," I said, flopping down onto my bed, absorbing the richness of his voice. "But I didn't see her today. I think she may be under the weather."

"Hmm. And I'm guessing she doesn't need any help from her trusty sidekick?" he asked.

"No – it's not even worth his effort," I told him, hating that I'd considered – even for a second – letting him rescue me. Whatever had been said or written about me that week was partially my fault, so I had to suck up the consequences, like it or not. I didn't want Taiton, Brandon, or anyone else fighting my battles.

After Taiton and I hung up, I couldn't concentrate on

my homework, and instead kept flipping back and forth between the short descriptive paragraph I was supposed to write: (*Begin the first sentence with a prepositional phrase ...*) and my E-Me page. Then, when Daphne needed belly rubs, and I was feeling totally drained, I lay down on the couch with her on the floor beside me.

It was after seven and completely dark outside when Dad got home and found me there, sleeping.

"Hey," he said. I sat up, disoriented.

"Hey, Dad."

"So you're still not feeling very well," he said, rubbing my back the way he used to when I was little.

I yawned and stretched before rolling over again on to my side. "I just need a little more sleep," I muttered.

And, because he's my dad, he let me sleep. Which is how I found myself at school the following day without having completed my homework for the first time in my school career. Lots of kids showed up every day without their homework, but not me. Not when my mother expected nothing but the best effort from her daughter, whatever the circumstances (even cancer!). I almost felt like I was going to make a headline on the front page of the school paper: "Pigs Fly! Money Grows on Trees! Hell Freezes Over! Ashley Skips Her Homework!" Or worse, on

E-Me. I could just see the gossip: **Did you hear about Ashley? She doesn't do her homework anymore because she spends all of her time IN BED!**

But a part of me recognized that I *had* been legitimately sick, and probably still was, because everything felt fuzzy and it was hard to focus. The energizers didn't feel energizing anymore, but I'd also gone several nights in a row without any sleep aids. It occurred to me that maybe I wasn't getting as much of a quality rest without them.

Back at school, I planned to catch up by going to the library during lunchtime. But somehow, I felt like hanging out with Taiton calmed me down, and I found myself not wanting to leave his side. When I was with him, I didn't have to concentrate, because he'd be on to a new topic before I'd digested the old one. Then, too, I was reluctant to leave the cafeteria without him. I was afraid I'd hear whispers or catch looks. People might wonder what he and I were doing together. But at least they couldn't attack me in his company.

And when Mr. Campbell, my English teacher, came around looking for the paragraph he had assigned the day before, he hardly even looked at my desk, at first. Likely it was because my work had always been done in the past, and he just assumed it would be done that day. Then he glanced down, his eyes grew wide, and he made eye contact with me. I looked down and pressed my lips together between my teeth, feeling my face get hot, because even though I'd kind of *decided* it didn't matter, I wasn't ready to admit it out loud. To my surprise, Mr. Campbell bent over and whispered in my ear. "You're a good student, and I know your mom's not well. Don't worry about this." Then he smiled at me as if he'd just given me a gift. I sat there, trying to appreciate it, but failing miserably.

# CHAPTER 12

I stayed with my dad for the rest of the week, resting my voice, sleeping in, popping into the animal shelter only once, and doing minimal schoolwork. I told myself I was taking a break because I'd been so run down that I'd gotten sick. But in reality, I just didn't have the energy to focus on anything. No matter what combination of medications I took, I felt both jumpy and distracted. So I alternated between energizers and Calm-Its, trying to find a balance that would make me feel okay.

Caitlyn had left me a voice mail and followed up with an e-mail as soon as she'd discovered the E-Me catastrophe:

> **OMG, Ashley. I am SO SORRY!!!!! I was trying to be funny when I wrote that stuff, and I never meant it to turn it into something so ugly. I hope you can forgive me. My horoscope said I should think before**

**I act, and I figured that had something to do with Conner (which is a whole other thing) but it was probably really a warning not to go commenting on other people's pics. I hope you are okay – let me know if anything's new with Taiton.**

I knew she was completely sincere when she apologized, and I didn't want her to worry. It wasn't like she'd purposely set me up, so I wrote back, telling her not to stress and deliberately downplaying the extent of the problem. I said nothing about the note in the locker because it would have just made her feel worse. I was having enough trouble keeping up with school, the shelter, rehearsals, and my mom – who was about to have more chemo – anyway. In the grand scheme of my life, a little E-Me gossip really wasn't feeling like such a big deal anymore.

As for Taiton, I told her only what I knew: he seemed to like me, but for a guy who was reputed to get around, he was showing incredible restraint – so it was possible that I was misreading his signals. I told myself that he was basically just a touchy-feely person, so it wasn't necessarily significant that he put his hand on the small of my back, below the hem of my shirt, when we walked together.

There *were* things I could do to test his feelings, or push the relationship – if that was what it was – into new territory. But as much as I thought about kissing him, I didn't know if I had the time or the energy for a boyfriend. Besides, if I had to ask for his affection, or have a big talk about where we stood, what was the point? Anything he said after that would feel forced.

By the beginning of the next week, my voice – if not my energy – had recovered, the *Camelot* sets were almost finished, and the cast had been instructed to wear their costumes around school all day for Halloween.

At Caitlyn's earlier suggestion, and with Mom's blessing, I'd altered the dress from her third wedding. She'd already let me wear it for Halloween the year before, and the fit was perfect. By adding colored ribbons in a few strategic places, and topping my hair with a plastic tiara, I managed to make the ensemble a bit less bridal and, I thought, a lot more regal.

Taiton, like all of the guys in the show, was wearing tights for his costume. The muscles in his thin legs were prominent under the close-fitting material. I noticed girls doing double-takes when they saw him. Finally, he had an excuse for his ceaseless movements, and all day long he leapt and twirled like a ballerina.

"Dance with me, my Queen," he begged, as he got down on one knee in front of the cafeteria.

"T'would not be proper, m'Lord," I replied in my best Guinevere voice. But still, he spun me around and dipped me a few times before swooping me up in his arms and marching me into the cafeteria like a bride over the threshold.

The bridal imagery was not lost on those who witnessed it, as I discovered later that afternoon.

Since I wasn't really a bride, I didn't have any bridesmaids to help me with the heavy crinoline under the dress, and going to the washroom in a tiny stall was more complicated than I'd expected. I'd been in the stall for a while when a couple of other girls entered the washroom and began to gossip.

"I heard she lost her voice from making out with a bunch of guys at the party," one of them said, "Why else would her supposed best friend be making comments about her spreading it around?"

"I don't know about that," the other voice said. "But she's *definitely not* a virgin bride! I heard the reason Brandon broke up with her was that she was seeing a couple of models over the summer, behind his back. Anyway, everyone knows Taiton's been with half the school."

"Yeah, but he's hot – you can't blame her for doing him."

As the door swung shut behind them, I found myself torn between fascination and disbelief. If my brain hadn't felt so foggy, I might have moved quickly enough to see who they were and set them straight. But by the time I maneuvered my dress out of the stall, they were already gone and the hall was empty. I went back in the stall and began to vomit, over and over again, the way my mom did after chemo.

When it stopped, my nose and throat tasted sour and burned from the inside out, the way shame seemed to burn into my every thought. I couldn't believe I had ever worried about being considered a goody-good. I would have given anything to recover that reputation. I wasn't going to get Brandon involved, but I wished, not for the first time, that Taiton carried a cell. There were things I needed to talk to him about, but I was too ashamed to show my face in the halls.

I waited until after the bell had signaled the beginning of last period, and then I dropped a note in his locker, and made my way down the hall to the office, where I signed myself out. I still wasn't prepared to go to the teachers about whoever was dissing me so wrongly. And what evidence did I have to go on anyway? It wasn't like I knew who'd said it. But I was ready, finally, to admit that ignoring it wasn't working. It was time to go home and talk to my mom about it.

* * *

I expected to find her in bed, or hunched over the toilet. Instead, I found her flushed and flustered, rummaging around in the bathroom.

"What are you looking for?" I asked. Normally, she could find anything within seconds.

"The thermometer," she said. "I think I might have a bit of a fever."

Just putting my hand on her cheek told me she was right. Mom's immunity was already low from the chemo. I knew that if she'd caught my virus, it could get much worse for her.

My own problems evaporated as I ran a washcloth under cold water and handed it to her. "I'm so sorry," I said in a wobbly voice.

"Why on earth would you think this was your fault?" she asked, setting the washcloth aside and putting her arm on my shoulder.

"Because I was sick ..."

"Ashley – listen to me – you had that virus two weeks ago! I've been out for chemo and blood work. I could have caught it from anyone. And even if it is from your cold, so what? It's not like you did it on purpose!"

"I just ... I just want you to get better," I said.

"I *will* get better, Ashley. I believe that."

"I know," I said, burying my head in her shoulder, and my problems in the back of my mind. Because even though she'd rejected so many of the alternative remedies I'd offered, the one thing that she'd always believed in was the power of positive thinking.

* * *

I left our Halloween candy with a neighbor and posted a sign asking trick-or-treaters not to ring the doorbell, then tried to get Mom settled for the night.

"What's up?" Taiton asked when, in response to the note I'd left in his locker, he called later that evening.

The gossip I'd heard in the washroom seemed far away and almost unreal next to my concern for Mom's well being. I didn't even bother mentioning it to him.

"I just had to leave early because of some stuff with

my mom," I explained. "Can you let Mrs. Emrich know that I might not be in tomorrow? But, you know, without making it into a big deal?"

"Not a problem," he said. And I knew that for him, it wouldn't be. I tried to remember a time when I, too, had felt competent and in control. But like my mother's health and my reputation, any sense of my competence seemed to have slipped away.

I stayed home to be with Mom while her fever hovered between "probably nothing to worry about" and "maybe we should call the doctor." While she was stuck in bed feeling crappy, I was trapped in my own personal hell, wanting to help but not knowing how.

I plumped pillows and offered food. But while I'd been at Dad's, she'd started drinking canned vitamin- and mineral-enriched shakes in chocolate, strawberry, and vanilla flavors, and I couldn't convince her to try anything else. They were better than nothing, but I thought she'd get more vitamins from real food.

"I can still use the juicer to whip up a fruity concoction," I offered the first time she'd asked for one of the shakes. "And I'll even sneak in some vegetables if you want."

"Thanks, sweetie," she said, "but I'm having trouble

with juice. I think I've developed some of those mouth sores they warned me about, and I don't want to aggravate the problem with anything acidic." So, it wasn't just the metallic taste in her mouth and the lack of appetite that had altered her diet yet again.

On Friday evening, Mom's fever suddenly spiked. She was incredibly weak, and when she tried standing so she could get to the bathroom, she admitted that her chest felt tight. Against her wishes, I called Dad. He came right over and declared that it was time to go to the emergency room.

"I'll probably just catch something worse there," Mom argued, albeit weakly.

"Or you'll get treatment for whatever the problem is," I said. Together, Dad and I walked her out to his car and got her to the hospital.

"It's pneumonia," the doctor said after examining her.

"Did she get it because I had a cold?" I asked, my legs feeling wobbly.

"Not necessarily," the doctor explained. "But her immune system has definitely been weakened by the drugs and stress." Although I was being told that it wasn't my fault, I had trouble believing it.

"So what happens next?" Dad asked the doctor.

"I'd like to keep her in, at least for a few days, to run

some IV antibiotics," the doctor said.

It was after midnight, and Mom was sleeping in her hospital bed by the time Dad and I got up to see her and say goodnight. Her bald head was smooth against the pillow, but one arm was crowded with tape and tubes connecting her to a bag of clear fluids. There was a blood pressure monitor attached to the finger of her other hand. Seeing her there like that pushed my own heart rate into overdrive. I got so hot and dizzy that I had to sit down in the visitor's chair and catch my breath.

It was hard to leave her there alone. It was even harder not knowing when she'd be released.

"It's late," Dad said, as we pulled into his driveway. "And your mother's in good hands. Try to sleep in tomorrow."

I nodded, knowing I'd need to.

"I'll check on your mom in the morning before I go to work," he said, "and you can sleep in. When you get up, maybe head back to her house and pack some things. Then I can pick you up at noon and take you to see her."

"What about Raven?" I asked, clenching my hands so tightly that my fingernails dug into my palms. "I already fed her for the night, but I don't want to leave her all alone there indefinitely ..."

"You can give her breakfast when you stop by in the morning, and we'll figure something out after we know more about your mother," he said.

I knew he was right. And I had many, many other things to still figure out.

# CHAPTER 13

Without having been able to pack, I had to make do at Dad's without my sleep aids. I don't know whether it was because of worrying about Mom or because I kept remembering what I'd heard in the bathroom at school, but I couldn't sleep at all.

Not seeing any point in lying awake in bed, I got up early the next morning.

Dad was already up. "I just got off the phone with the hospital," he said when I came down for breakfast. "Your mom's had a good night, and she's resting comfortably. She doesn't have a telephone yet, but she should later on today."

I felt my body loosen in areas I didn't realize had been tense. "I'm glad she's okay," I said. "I didn't really sleep much."

Dad exhaled loudly and shook his head. "To be honest, neither did I. But this is not a major problem.

I'm sure this is just a little bump in the road to your mom's recovery."

"I know," I said.

"The hospital doesn't want visitors until after noon. So what are we going to do with our morning?"

I'd been thinking about that all night. "I have to go back and feed Raven," I said. "And pack, in case I'm here for a while." I didn't tell him that I wanted – needed – the energizers as much as I needed to pick up clean underwear.

Dad didn't argue. He knew me well enough to understand that I'd be more comfortable doing something productive, like packing and feeding cats, than hanging around for a leisurely breakfast.

When I got to Mom's, Raven meowed and rubbed against my legs. I made feeding her my first priority, and getting hold of my vitamins and energizers second. Then, feeling a bit more alert, I packed for a couple of days. All my years of alternating between two houses had made me an expert at packing and organization. But several times that morning, I found myself staring into the closet or dresser drawers, forgetting what I needed or was looking for. Everything felt brighter, louder, and sharper than usual. It didn't help that I had so many things racing through my mind that I couldn't focus on anything.

When I went to Mom's room to get some things for her, I thought maybe she'd like her MP3 player, so I went back down the kitchen to find it. That somehow led me to watering the plants and scrubbing the sink with an old toothbrush. Then I went back upstairs to pack Mom's toothbrush. I went around and around like that, happy to have the energy, but unable to focus. Even choosing a nightgown or a bathrobe became an impossible task.

When I finally finished, I had two bags ready to go and several hours left until Dad picked me up. I still had homework to do, but there was no way I could concentrate on it. I convinced myself that since my teachers had been understanding the last time I showed up unprepared, they wouldn't be upset if, with Mom in the hospital, I repeated the transgression.

At about nine in the morning, my telephone rang. It was Taiton.

"How's it going?" he asked.

I filled him in, and then asked him how rehearsal had gone without me.

"How about if I come over and tell you?" he asked, as I imagined his lanky body leaping through the front door. "I'll bring coffee."

True to his word, he arrived within twenty minutes

with two lattes in hand. I reached for mine, gratefully, and felt an intense rush as my fingers brushed his. As the fridge hummed behind me, I realized that we were truly alone together for the first time ever. I knew what that would mean to the gossipers at school, but I didn't have any idea what it would mean to us. My brain went through a dozen scenarios in seconds. Taiton led me over to the sofa and took my free hand in his, which startled me a bit.

"You okay?" he asked warily. "You're jumpier than me today."

"I'm just ... a little disoriented," I admitted. "I'm trying to get ready to go to my dad's for a while, and I didn't sleep very well."

He nodded, and tucked my hair back behind my ear, but I got the sense that he didn't really believe me.

"So I heard some stuff at rehearsal the other day," he began. I blushed and looked away, remembering what the girls in the washroom had said.

"Like?" I waited for the worst of it.

"Like, Mrs. Emrich would normally be furious with a lead actor who missed as many rehearsals as you have lately. But she's totally okay with you because you have all of your lines and music down so perfectly that you'd probably be ready to go on tomorrow. She said the rest of us would do well to follow your example and learn our stuff."

"Really?" Relief flooded over me – though I felt guilty for all of the rehearsals I'd missed. Still, I hoped that that was all he'd heard.

"And truly." He bounced his knee up and down while he spoke. "Well, except for me, because I know my lines too. And yours. And, well, everyone else's. I think she kind of lumps us together."

*Like a couple,* I thought, watching his face. He smiled back at me the same way he always did. I didn't have the nerve to say aloud what I was thinking. What everyone at school was probably thinking too. And maybe that was a good thing, because it would be nice for something in my life to be uncomplicated for a change.

I knew he was waiting for a response from me, so I inched my way through the rush of sounds and electricity that seemed to buzz around me. "How did the rest of the cast react to Mrs. Emrich's speech?" I asked, still concerned that people were talking about me as if I was a slut.

"Ryan agreed that you're doing a great job, but blamed your absences for his failure to learn all of his lines," he admitted. "Then Shelby pointed out that he mostly stumbles when he does his scenes with Merlin, and since Merlin is his girlfriend, maybe they should spend more time rehearsing together and less time doing whatever else it is that they actually do."

"She did not!" My voice was louder than I intended, and Taiton jumped. I tried to think back to the voices I'd heard in the girls' washroom, and wondered whether Shelby might have been one of them. I didn't think so, but I hadn't ever seen that side of her before. "How did Mrs. Emrich react to that?"

"She said she didn't know about that, but that since you and I have our parts down, maybe everyone should do whatever it is *we're* doing."

"And?"

"And then everyone laughed, and Mrs. Emrich blushed, and told us to get back to work," he grinned.

"What *are* we doing?" I asked, feeling confused. I wanted to give him a sense that I was open to suggestion. But I knew this would forever change whatever it was that we already had. Maybe he was also afraid of changing the comfortable buzz between us. Or maybe he didn't feel it the way I did. Either way, it wasn't time for me to know.

"Not nearly as much as some people seem to think," he said, giving me a wink that told me it was okay. No matter what he'd heard – and he obviously *had* heard something – he wasn't judging. "So what I think we should do is ..."

"Get to the hospital to see my mom," I finished. Knowing that he was there for me – whether romantically, or just as a friend – in spite of the rumors, was enough. At this point, I just wanted to be there for my mom.

As always, he accepted my sudden change of plans without a word. And I thought, as he gave me his hand to help me up from the couch, that I might actually love him.

* * *

"Sing to me," he said later, swaying rhythmically back and forth in front of the hospital's elevator.

I'd popped a couple of Calm-Its before we'd left, and they seemed to be moderating the crazy energy I'd had earlier. "Sing? Here? Now?" I looked around at an orderly pushing a cart full of clean linens, and wondered what had brought on the request. "Why?"

"You're going to be performing for an entire auditorium in just six weeks. And," he added, his own voice taking on a musical cadence, "I believe it was Maria in *The Sound of Music* who sang that she always felt better when she remembered her favorite things. So why not sing here, where people could use a little cheering up? Come on – the simple folk would do it."

"Why not?" I agreed, encouraged by the way he alluded to Guinevere's song about being glum, and knowing he understood that I was the one who really needed the cheering up.

Once I began, I found that he was right. Despite the odd circumstances, my mood seemed to lift with my voice as I sang in the hallways of the building.

The elevator door slid open, revealing a little old man and his blue-haired wife standing side by side, holding hands. I hesitated just for a second, but then continued as the elevator doors closed behind us. At the third floor, the old couple shuffled off smiling at me, and a man in a hospital gown, pushing an IV pole, got on. At the fifth floor, Taiton began singing with me, joining in with King Arthur's part in a rich smooth baritone that I hadn't known he possessed.

I wanted to stop and exclaim that he had never told me he could sing, and that he should have tried out for one of the leads. But I was afraid that pointing it out would make him stop, and I wanted nothing more than to keep singing with him, so I reached for his hand. The man with the IV stayed on, even though he had already passed his floor. A woman carrying a screaming toddler and pushing a baby in a stroller looked at us, bewildered but grateful, as Taiton helped maneuver the stroller in without missing a note. The toddler sniffed and hiccupped, but stopped crying, either distracted or enchanted.

It was one of the first times in my life that I'd ever *not* worried about how I'd look or what people might think, and it felt great.

We finished the song as we arrived at my mom's room, and found her in bed, smiling dreamily.

"You two sound wonderful together," she said, kissing my cheek as I bent down to her. She had shadows under her eyes, and her voice was little more than a whisper. "I can't wait to see the show. I'm so proud of you. You know that, right? You know that I'm proud of you?"

My mother had never been one for grand emotional displays. I'd always known she loved me, and I always knew she'd be proud of me as long as I was doing my best. But, unlike my dad, she rarely made a point of saying so. I squeezed her hand, being careful not to touch her IV, and reassured her that of course I knew.

"I can't wait for you to see it, either," I told her excitedly. "This place," I said, peering around the sparse room, "is definitely not Camelot."

Taiton went home shortly after, and I stayed with Mom through the afternoon. Mostly, she slept, but I was glad to be there whenever she woke up. Just like when I'd been sick and she'd been there for me. I remembered how comforting I found that. That was the feeling I wanted to give her.

Mom drifted in and out of sleep while I sat, trying yet again – and still without success – to do some homework. My body had settled down from my early morning energy rush, but I still felt like I was watching movie clips in fast forward. Reading, which had always been something I enjoyed, was becoming increasingly difficult. The words seemed to jump around the page. I couldn't even get past the first few paragraphs of the chapter I'd been assigned. I wondered how long my teachers would accept the excuse of a sick mother before I'd have to buckle down and do my work again. I also wondered whether I'd ever feel like I used to.

That weekend, Mom and I talked about what we liked about *Camelot*.

"Honestly? I always thought that Guinevere was very lucky to have had two great loves," Mom confided. "Some people never even experience one."

"A whole kingdom is destroyed because of her

relationship with Lancelot, though," I argued. "It doesn't seem very lucky to me."

"No, that's not quite how it went," she argued, and I was glad she still had some fight in her. "The kingdom wasn't destroyed because of Guinevere and Lancelot's love. It came apart because of Mordred's meddling. Arthur was prepared to be silent about it, for the common good. But once Mordred spreads tales of her infidelity, everything gets out of control."

"So what's the ultimate moral of the story?" I asked her.

"I don't think there really is one," she whispered. "Only the possibility that perfection can exist again."

I thought a lot that weekend about how Mom had raised me – to always try my hardest, and do my best. To strive for perfection. And I thought about Arthur's struggle to keep his kingdom together, even with his heart broken, because doing the right thing and maintaining order was more important to him than seeking revenge.

I took the Calm-Its to slow my racing heart and take the edge off my anxiety over Mom. But I also made a conscious decision that I wasn't going to worry anymore about the odd stories that had surfaced about me.

I'd long since given up on posting anything on E-Me, but I did still check it regularly, just in case. And when I saw, day after day, that whoever had been spreading rumors about me in the washroom hadn't bothered to go public with their speculation, I assumed that it had all been forgotten by everyone – everyone but me.

# CHAPTER 14

In the days that followed Mom's hospitalization, everyone at school seemed to be moving slowly, in some kind of pre-winter fog. I'd worked out a combination of supplements that kept me energized but not frantic, letting me float between school, rehearsal, the shelter, the hospital, and Dad's house.

I couldn't seem to catch up on my homework, but for the most part, my teachers continued to give me special consideration. I told myself I'd catch up again after the musical. Like King Arthur, I did everything I could to present a façade of normalcy, trying not to worry my parents or provoke my castmates.

But sometimes, I found myself forgetting my lines – the same lines I'd nailed a month earlier. Mrs. Emrich dismissed it as an insignificant blip in the learning curve – one that I would surely get over before we opened in December.

By the time the art students were asked to create

posters advertising the show, I'd convinced myself (and everyone around me) that everything in my life was under control.

The cast was asked to pose for digital photos in our costumes. Some of the kids studying photography and graphic design took individual and group shots of us.

"Does this make you miss modeling?" Taiton whispered as I posed with him and Ryan. Ryan's cologne propelled me into a fit of sneezing before I could answer, making me feel anything but glamorous.

"No, but I miss Caitlyn a lot right now," I confessed. "She loves artsy stuff."

"Like Conner?" he grinned, teasing me gently about the little bits of info I'd shared about their budding relationship.

"Yes – like Conner," I said. Then, trying to throw him a hint, I said, "I'm glad they decided to follow their hearts."

"Maybe they didn't decide, but fate did." Taiton suggested, sounding very much like King Arthur. "Maybe passion can't be selected."

"Maybe," I sighed, wondering whether I'd ever work up the nerve to just kiss him. "But it can definitely be denied."

* * *

The posters went up about a week later. Each of the art students had designed their own, with the results as varied as the people who created them. Some featured the whole cast in full color, while others used monochromatic schemes, black and white, or sepia to create different moods and effects.

My favorite was one of Destiny, dressed in her wizard's outfit, with the headline, "Fall under the spell of *Camelot*!"

I was standing by my locker, telling her about how much I liked it, and thinking about how far the two of us had come as castmates and friends, when Taiton and Brandon approached me. It was more than unusual to see them together, and Destiny must have sensed from their solemn faces that something serious was up. She excused herself, and left the three of us alone.

"I'm sorry, Ash, but you need to see this," Brandon announced grimly, handing me a poster.

The photograph was of me in my Guinevere costume, with my hair tightly curled and piled high on my head. My eyes were closed, my mouth wide open, and my head tossed back at such an angle that a generous amount of cleavage was on display. I recognized immediately that the photo must have been taken mid-sneeze, courtesy of Ryan's overbearing cologne. But anyone who didn't know the context might think differently, because of the accompanying text. A large headline proclaimed. "*CAMELOT*! Where the queen is hot ... and bothered." Underneath, in smaller letters, it said, "Call for private shows."

"Where ... where did you find this?" I stammered, feeling hot and dizzy.

"In the guys' locker room," Brandon replied. "But I've been coming across similar kinds of trash for a while, so I went to Taiton first, thinking maybe he had something to do with it."

"He wouldn't ..." I said, starting to defend him.

"He knows," Taiton said, delicately brushing his fingers along my neck in a way that suggested that surely we must be more than friends. "I told him about how I've been trying to extinguish the little fires of gossip for a while now, and about how stubborn you've been about accepting any help."

"And as soon as he mentioned your stubborn independence, I knew he was telling the truth," Brandon grinned, despite the situation.

My head was still spinning as Taiton continued. "So even though we both love that you're crazy and independent, we want to help."

"No," I said, trying to clear my head, and folding the poster into my backpack. "I don't want to be rescued. I'm going to take care of it myself."

I stopped at the water fountain on my way to class and took out some Calm-Its, but I was shaking so hard that they spilled onto the floor. As I picked them up, I wondered whether the eyes I felt watching me were because I'd dropped something, or because they had seen the poster too. There was no way of knowing how many copies might be circulating and thinking about it made me sick to my stomach.

I was still thinking about how to handle the poster when Principal Weeber showed up at the classroom door.

# CHAPTER 15

"Ashley," he said, "come with me, please. And bring your things."

I'd never been sent to the principal's office. And I'd certainly never had him come down personally to get me. At first, I figured he must know about the posters, and I felt embarrassed as we made the long, silent walk down the hall to his office.

But when we came around the corner and I saw my dad sitting there, I was certain that my worst fears had come true. Something terrible had happened to my mother.

I cried out, gasping, as my father stood up.

"Ashley, what's wrong?" he asked, grabbing me before I could fall.

"You tell me ..." I said, as if choking on something in my throat.

"I have no idea!" he said. "The school just called, and said I needed to come down."

"But Mom's okay?" I sniffed, still confused by his presence.

"Your mother's fine," Dad assured me. "And you?"

"Maybe I can clear this up," Principal Weeber interrupted, and we both stared, remembering that he was there. "I got a tip today from one of the students suggesting that Ashley has been using drugs here at school." He turned to face me directly. His face and tone were neutral, so even though I was horrified, I couldn't tell whether he believed what he was saying or not. "I have spoken with several of your teachers, Ashley, and they did confirm that your work habits have been inconsistent, and that you often seem to be 'out of it.'"

I felt the blood drain from my face, and every part of my body tensed up. I hoped it didn't make me look guilty because surely, if he'd mentioned drugs, Principal Weeber was still looking for evidence. Dad was sitting quietly, but he'd drawn his eyebrows together, and leaned slightly forward in his chair.

"Now, obviously, those are very serious accusations, with potential legal implications," Principal Weeber said. "Which," he turned to my dad, "is why I asked you to come today."

Always my champion, Dad stepped in to respond to

the accusations: "And I'm certainly glad that you called, Principal Weeber. Ashley has been under a lot of stress at home during the past couple of months. I'm quite certain that stress will account for her performance and her behavior. My daughter doesn't do drugs. So if you have nothing more?"

I clenched and unclenched my fists as Principal Weeber smiled apologetically.

"Given your home situation, it seems perfectly reasonable that we would be noticing changes at school," Principal Weeber said. "So I don't really believe we have an issue here, either. But I do have a duty to investigate. Ashley, if you'd be willing to open your backpack and let us see its contents, I think that would suffice."

"I don't have drugs ..." I stammered, unzipping my bag, and pulling things out. "Just vitamins and stuff from the health food store."

One by one, out came the sleep aids, the energizers, the Calm-Its, and a couple of bottles of vitamins. I was infuriated that they were making me look like an addict needing a fix. I lined them up on Principal Weeber's desk so he – and Dad – could see that I had absolutely nothing to hide.

"See? They're all natural ..."

Dad's eyes opened wide as he grabbed one of the bottles and began reading the label. Principal Weeber examined another, and they glanced at one another before turning back to me.

"Ashley – aren't these what you bought for your mother? *You* haven't been taking all this stuff, have you?"

"Well – sometimes. Like when I can't sleep or I can't wake up." I realized how insane the words sounded as soon as they came out of my mouth.

Principal Weeber sat back in his chair. Dad knelt in front of me, with one of the bottles in his hand. "Sweetheart – even if they're legal and natural, they're still drugs that can alter your mood or behavior." He brushed a tear from my eye. "It can't be good for you to be taking these in any combination. I'd noticed you looking a little glassy-eyed lately, but I thought you were just upset about things at home. You could have made yourself very ill ... but you haven't done anything you should be punished for." He glanced back at Principal Weeber, as if to double-check that what he'd just told me was accurate.

Principal Weeber smiled graciously, then allowed his concern to return to his face. "If you could look into these supplements," he said to my dad, "I don't see any reason to take formal action. But Ashley, it might be wise if you consulted with your family doctor, just to make sure you're okay."

I was embarrassed at my stupidity and certain that by now, a whole new set of "dope-fiend" rumors must be circulating. There didn't seem to be any way out. The idea that the rumors would never end and that there was nothing I could do to stop them overwhelmed me to tears.

# CHAPTER 16

"Ashley?" my dad asked gently, after he and Principal Weeber had let me cry for a moment. "Didn't you hear us? You're not in trouble."

"It won't matter," I said, trying to steady my breathing and control my voice. "Because they'll still say it's true. The next time I'm absent, they'll make up stories about me being suspended, or they'll say I did something disgusting to get off the hook."

"What are you talking about?" my dad asked. "Who's 'they,' and why would 'they' make up stories?"

I didn't answer right away. I prided myself on my independence, and my ability to solve my own problems. So telling my dad and the principal about the rumors was as hard as dealing with them.

But it was something I knew I needed to do. I had to accept that sometimes I couldn't handle everything on my own.

"I don't know who 'they' are," I acknowledged. "Probably whoever told Principal Weeber I was on drugs. And I don't know why they're doing it, but they've been making up stuff about me all year. I tried to deal with it myself, but it just won't stop."

"What kind of rumors are we talking about?" Principal Weeber asked quietly.

I couldn't look either one of them in the eye as I explained, so I focused on the toe of my right shoe. "Lots of things. That I shouldn't be in the musical. But also that I'm a slut, that I – do things – for personal gain. Sometimes they say it behind my back, but sometimes they put it in writing too." I pulled the *Camelot* flyer out of my jeans pocket and unfolded it for them to see. Principal Weeber must have been used to dealing with stuff like that, but my dad's face went gray when he saw it.

"It's not true, Dad," I said, suddenly more worried about him than me. "It's just a bunch of lies." As humiliating as it was to have my own father looking at the crude poster of his only daughter, just acknowledging out loud that it was a load of crap made me feel better in ways I hadn't expected.

Once I'd stopped crying, I told them the whole story. Dad and Principal Weeber listened carefully, asking for clarification only when necessary. When I was finished, I felt more exhausted than ever, but I knew I wouldn't need any more energizers, because I had already started feeling lighter and more in control.

"Thank you for bringing this to our attention, Ashley," Principal Weeber said. "Let me assure you both that there will be no further incidents of this sort."

"Let's head home, sweetie," Dad said, taking my bag. "We can fill your mother in about what's been going on."

"If it's okay with you, Dad, I'd rather stay. After everyone seeing me get hauled out of class I really need to be here. Plus, I've missed enough rehearsals. I'll talk to Mom, but if you don't mind, I'd like to wait a little longer ... just until everything settles down a bit." I wasn't afraid of her reaction – I just wanted to keep her stress level down while she recovered from pneumonia.

"Okay," he agreed, rubbing my back affectionately. Despite their marital differences when they'd been together, the one thing Mom and Dad had always agreed on was keeping a united front when it came to parenting. They didn't keep things concerning me from each other. But this situation was different, because it was about Mom's health and her well-being. His willingness to hold off telling Mom meant he still trusted me. And that meant more than anything my schoolmates thought.

I went to rehearsal, ignoring the usual flurry of stares and whispers that followed me.

We were just finishing up when Principal Weeber came in and asked to speak with Ryan.

# CHAPTER 17

It turned out that Ryan – my "husband" in the show – admitted both to starting the rumors and to making the posters.

"It seems that he was upset about his girlfriend not getting your role," Principal Weeber explained to me the next day. "After I spoke with the art class about who had access to the pictures they'd taken, it was fairly easy to track down the digital file of the posters, which Ryan had created in the computer lab. I've also spoken with Destiny, and checked her school account. I believe her when she says she had no idea what he'd been up to."

Principal Weeber suspended Ryan, banned him from using the school computers, and forbade him from having any contact with me. Ultimately, that meant he got tossed from the show.

I should have felt better, but I was afraid that the entire cast would hate me more than Ryan apparently had.

We were set to perform in only two weeks' time, and we'd just lost our King Arthur.

"It looks as though we'll have to postpone the production until after the holidays," Mrs. Emrich explained without mentioning the reason for the delay, but obviously having a hard time keeping her gaze off me. My face burned, knowing that she – and possibly everyone else – might somehow feel that I'd overreacted.

"In the meantime," she continued, "we'll recast, and focus on bringing a new Arthur up to speed."

Taiton squeezed my hand and muttered a line from the play describing how much everyone had been through for nothing more than an idea.

"Taiton can do it," I said, thinking clearly, and feeling determined, for the first time in months.

"Excuse me?"

"King Arthur," I said. "Taiton can play the king with his eyes closed. He already knows all the lines, and he sings like a Broadway star. If you give him the part, we can go on as scheduled."

"Taiton? Is that true? Do you think you're up to this?" Mrs. Emrich asked.

"But what about Pellinore?" Destiny asked, and I hurt for her, knowing that she had to suffer the humiliation of her boyfriend being dismissed from the play. "King Pellinore's never on stage without King Arthur. Taiton can't play both roles – we're *still* going to need somebody else."

"You can be Pellinore," I said quickly, turning to face Destiny. Taiton squeezed my hand again. "You'd be great at it. Merlin and Pellinore don't have any scenes together, and your talent deserves more of a showcase than just the one role," I said. "And you won't have any trouble learning Pellinore's lines."

Hoping to head off speculation that I was acting out of personal regard for Taiton, I turned to my fellow cast members. "My mom's been doing chemo for breast cancer, and seeing the show would mean a lot to her. I'd like to keep on schedule if we can."

Then, the most remarkable thing happened. Instead of all the looks of pity I'd been dreading, I found myself staring back at a group of friends with caring faces. Friends who clearly wanted to help and couldn't believe I hadn't shared such an important part of my life earlier. Friends who probably understood how hard it was for me to discuss this openly. It suddenly seemed ridiculous, given all of the embarrassing (and completely untrue) stuff that had been said about me, that I would have even hesitated to say anything about the one thing in my life that mattered most.

Mrs. Emrich beamed with pleasure, as if she'd thought of everything all by herself. "Well?"

"Well ... I'm already playing one old guy. I guess I could do two parts," Destiny conceded.

"Taiton?"

Taiton leaped onto the stage and crowed in character: "I'll not just be a king – I'll be the king of *Camelot*!" The cast applauded wildly. The dream of *Camelot* was once again alive with possibility.

"That was awesome!" Taiton said later, leaning his forehead down to touch mine. "My queen."

After twenty-four hours without supplements, I was thinking more clearly, even though I was sweaty and shaking. The doctor I had seen yesterday had said that the physical symptoms – a withdrawal of some kind – would pass with time.

Now, with the fog lifted from my mind, I couldn't believe – even as stubbornly independent as I was – that I hadn't sought help for the bullying earlier.

I took a deep breath, and told Taiton what I'd been waiting months to say. "You know those things people were saying about me weren't true ..." I began.

He nodded. "I know."

"But I don't want you to think I'm a goody-good, either."

He shook his head, and gave me a lopsided grin. "I don't."

"But you could pretty much have any girl you want, and you've been with so many. Yet you've never tried anything with me?"

"Who told you I'd been with a lot of girls?" he asked softly.

I realized, right then, that nobody had. At least, nobody specific. It was just something I'd heard a few times, and assumed to be true because of his incredible good looks and magnetic personality.

"I'm sorry," I said, embarrassed at my own willingness to believe stories about someone else. "I just ... I thought maybe you liked me as more than the good friend you've been, but then I wasn't sure. I mean, if you had any romantic feelings for me, you showed a lot of self-restraint."

In response, he pulled me to him, ran his fingers through my hair, and kissed me long and deep.

"Wow," I gasped, as we finally came up for air. "I can't believe I didn't know how you felt ..."

"I try to be a civilized man," he said in character before kissing me again. "But I do have occasional lapses."

* * *

Mom got out of hospital the next day, still weak, but looking better than she had for a long time. And she was totally understanding about my misadventure with herbal supplements.

"That's part of what concerned me from the start," she said. "That they weren't regulated. I just wish I'd noticed what was going on with you."

"Don't blame yourself," I said, still headachey and nauseated from not taking the supplements anymore, and feeling like a total idiot as well. "I made some stupid, dangerous choices. You were right all along."

"The funny thing is," she smiled, "that my doctor at the hospital suggested I try some gentle yoga, to keep me more mobile so my lungs don't fill up with fluid again. She said yoga seems to be helpful in reducing the stress in cancer patients too. So even though the supplements didn't work out, it seems that you were right about some of the things you suggested. I'm sorry if I made you feel badly by dismissing all of them."

"I'm sorry I accused you of not fighting hard enough," I said, thinking about my own recent battles. "I understand now that sometimes it takes more strength to resist quietly than to kick and scream in protest."

Then, I changed the subject to a brighter topic. She was almost giddy when I told her the news that Taiton and I were officially a couple.

> So what actually took him so long? Caitlyn asked in a text message immediately after I filled her in.

>> He said he figured I needed a friend more than a boyfriend, I texted back. And I think he was right. But now I'm down one friend, so hurry back!

* * *

On opening night, we played to a packed house. Mom, Dad, and Gabriella had managed to score front-row seats. Although I wished Caitlyn could have been there, I knew she was rooting for me from Quebec.

Taiton shone as King Arthur. Backstage, people were saying that the musical was infinitely better with Taiton in the Arthur role. Even Destiny said so. I held my tongue, but I couldn't agree more.

Taiton brought the house to a standing ovation after he belted out his final lines about always trying to remember how brightly *Camelot* had shone, and all the good it had once inspired.

After the final curtain call, he grabbed a microphone from offstage and rejoined the company.

"I'd like to make a special announcement, if I may," he said, and the audience was quiet. "The entire cast has worked very hard this semester to make the musical a success. But one of our cast members has been working extra hard because she has a parent with cancer."

A light murmur of speculation began in the auditorium as Taiton continued, tactfully skirting my name. "This individual never asks for help, but the rest of the cast has talked about it, and we want to show our support for her and for her family. So we've decided as a cast – and as her friends – that the proceeds of tonight's performance will be donated to the Breast Cancer Foundation."

The audience burst into wild cheers and applause. I looked toward my mother and saw her face lined with tears. I struggled to keep my own composure, as Taiton pulled me forward, bent his knee with Arthurian gallantry, and presented me with a bouquet.

Once the curtain came down, I kissed him.

"Thank you," I said. "I never expected anything like that ..."

"Don't cry anymore," he said, smiling and brushing new tears off my cheeks. "I know it's hard for you when things don't go the way you expect them to, but sometimes you just have to enjoy the journey."

We can't always control the way our lives unfold, no matter how noble our intentions. Sometimes, we can't even control ourselves. But if we're fighting for the right things, there's always the promise that good will triumph. King Arthur learned this as he struggled to preserve his idyllic kingdom. So did I.

## Accolades & Awards for **Posing as Ashley**

"With the same sincerity as **Painting Caitlyn**,
Peters captures the fragility of the teenage soul ..."
– *School Library Journal*

"... an immediately likeable protagonist whose
desperate need to try to always please everyone else
will resonate with many readers."
– *CM: Canadian Review of Materials*

"... realistic descriptions of what goes on behind the scenes
in the fashion world ... an eye-opening account."
– *Resource Links*

"... straightforward, readable, and honest."
– *Montreal Review of Books*

"Ashley's fight for confidence and peace with herself
is nuanced and genuine ..."
– *Children's Literature*

**Winner, 2008 Elementary Teachers' Federation
of Ontario Writer's Award**

**Selected, Canadian Children's Book Centre's
"Best Books for Kids & Teens"**

## Accolades & Awards for **Painting Caitlyn**

"Peters clearly has her finger on the pulse of teenage dating ..." – *School Library Journal*

"Realistic and powerful ... will stay with readers long after the book is closed." – *KLIATT*

"... more than just a simple problem novel." – *Booklist*

"... a provocative story with an important message."
– *CM: Canadian Review of Materials*

**Selected, International Reading Association "Young Adults' Choices" List**

**Selected, American Library Association "YALSA Quick Picks for Reluctant Young Adult Readers"**

**Winner, Elementary Teachers' Federation of Ontario Writer's Award, Women's Program**

**Shortlisted, B.C. Teen Readers' Choice Stellar Book Award**

**Selected by the Maine Coalition to End Domestic Violence for the "Knowledge is Power" Program**

# Get a sneak peek!

Turn the page to read the first chapter of
Painting Caitlyn.

# CHAPTER 1

There are some things you can't admit to anybody: not to your parents, not to your friends, not even to yourself.

Maybe it's because saying it out loud, acknowledging it, makes it more real. And the more real it is, the more frightening it becomes.

That's how it was for me.

But eventually, the truth has to come out, and you have to take all the little bits and pieces of your life that didn't seem to matter by themselves, and pick them up again, and shake them around, and put them back together into one big picture. And then you have to look at it, and you have to be honest about what it really is.

And sometimes, you have to stand back a little to see that truth. My self-portrait is like that. I spent so much time working up close, examining, perfecting, critiquing the small details – the curve of my lips, the mole on my cheek, the curl of my hair – that I couldn't see what was really wrong, why it just didn't look right. Now I know.

In the end, it wasn't really about *me*: it was all about *him*.

* * *

I hadn't met Tyler yet when I found out that I was finally going to have a baby brother or sister.

I say "finally" not because I'd been waiting for one – I'd given up on that idea long ago – but because my mom had been trying for so long to get pregnant again, and it was a dream *she* wouldn't give up on.

With me, it was easy. Accidental, actually. She was twenty years old, in college, and she got pregnant with her boyfriend. They never got married or anything. My mom says he left because he was too young and immature to be a parent, and he gave her full custody, and that's why I never see him.

He ended up moving out to the West Coast right after I was born. I only met him once, when he was back here for a business trip and I was about four years old. But I was so little that I mostly just remember the restaurant where we met him, because it had a big goldfish pond with a waterfall right in the middle of the restaurant. I spent almost the whole time looking at the fish, so I don't really remember my dad. After lunch, we stopped at a pet store, and he got me a goldfish to take home. I named it "Goldie."

Goldie died pretty fast, and I cried for days, and I kept hoping my dad would come back and buy me a new fish. My mom kept cursing him for giving me a pet in the first place.

Anyway, that was the last time I saw my "real" dad. I used to ask my mom about him, but she'd always just tell me that he moved a lot, and she didn't know where he was. When I tried looking him up on the Internet one time, I got about a thousand hits for his name – everything from politicians to parolees – so I don't know how I'll ever track him down by myself.

But you can't miss somebody you don't really know, right?

Anyway, my mom married Mike, my stepfather, when I was seven, and they'd been trying to give me a little brother or sister ever since.

Even after they married, I still didn't call him "Dad."

Mike started going out with my mom when I was about four, and I mostly liked him, because he used to take me to the zoo and everything, but now I think he was just doing that to suck up to my mom, and make her think he was okay with having a kid around. I was excited when they got married, because I got to be a flower girl, and wear this lacy pink dress my mom picked out for me while I carried a basket of flowers down the aisle. I thought it was so cool that at the reception I asked my mom if she could have another wedding the next day.

My happiness quickly evaporated. When they left for the honeymoon, my mom said, "Kiss Daddy good-bye," and I realized they weren't taking me with them. I was so mad, I decided then and there that I was *never* going to call him anything except Mike. And I never did.

I think it hurt his feelings when I used his first name. Now that I'm older, I totally understand why they wouldn't have wanted a little kid like me tagging along with them on their honeymoon, but I'd called him Mike for so long that I couldn't really imagine calling him anything else.

It's weird, thinking about my mom having sex. First, she obviously did it with my real dad, probably sneaking around the way Tyler and I did, because she was still living at home. And then with Mike, she didn't actually say, "We had sex last night, and it was great," but she talked about how they were still "trying for a baby."

I didn't know why another baby was so important to her, but it was. I used to think maybe something was wrong with me – that I wasn't pretty enough, or smart enough, or maybe she'd wanted me to be a boy, but she said it wasn't that – it was just that she wanted more children, and she wanted to give Mike a child, and someday I'd understand.

So that kind of pissed me off too. That she wanted to give Mike a child. Didn't she already give him me? For all their talk over the past several years about how I'm his daughter, and he loves me like his own, why did he still need "a child of his own" with my mom? Like I'm not his, never will be, and his own would be so much better. Maybe he *thought* it would be better, but I doubted it. For one thing, Mike has really big ears, and so do his dad, and his brother, and all the other guys in his family. There was no way that he could have a kid and not pass on those ears. I figured I'd end up with a brother or sister who looked like Dumbo.

My mom and Mike tried a whole bunch of things to get pregnant. For the first couple of years, while my mom was still in her twenties, the doctors just kept telling them to "relax." Then, when nothing was happening, they went in for testing, and it turned out that my mom had some plugged tubes or something, so she had an operation to try to fix it. After that, she was really happy for a few months, waiting to heal and thinking it would work. But then another few months went by, and a few more, and she still didn't get pregnant. It got so bad that sometimes, if she was supposed to go to a party or something where she knew people would have babies, she'd make up some excuse not to go. She said it was too painful to see everyone else with their perfect little families.

As a last resort, they did *in vitro* – you know, test-tube babies. My mom took a whole bunch of drugs, and had needles every day, and then they took some of her eggs and some of Mike's – stuff – (I get so grossed out even thinking about it), and mixed it all around, and then put it back in my mom. And finally, it took. She was pregnant.

I couldn't sleep the night they told me. Long after I had gone to bed, I took out my sketchbook and tried to draw my new family. I started with what I already knew. I drew myself: skinny – almost on the scrawny side, according to some people – with shoulder length strawberry-blond hair, and round green eyes. A mole on my cheek. Not bad looking, but probably nothing special, either.

Then, a little apart from me, because it seemed like we weren't as close as we used to be, I added my mom: a slightly older, heavier version of me, with darker hair (which she stopped bleaching in case it was making her not get pregnant), and a deeper tan (from the tanning salon – but the spray on kind, not the one from a tanning bed, because she was afraid the light from a tanning bed was also making her not get pregnant).

Mike was next. He's super tall – way over six feet – with dark hair and eyes, a moustache, and, like I already said, huge ears.

I drew him in with his arm around my mom, because he's very protective of her. One time, when I was about nine, he grounded me for two weeks for marching around the house when my mom had a headache. To this day, I think the punishment was totally excessive. I mean, I didn't know she had a headache, and I was just a little kid – he could have just asked me to stop. I think my mom should have done something to help me get out of the grounding, but she just said, "He's your father, and you have to abide by what he says."

I tried to sketch a baby into the picture next. I put it between my mom and Mike, because it would be theirs, but I'd already put Mom and Mike so close together that I couldn't really make the baby fit. And I had no idea how to do its face. I just couldn't picture a baby in our family, and I've never been good at drawing things from my imagination.

Unfortunately, along with the news that my parents had finally conceived came the news that I had to get out of my bedroom. My room was the one closest to my parents', so it had to be the nursery. They were going to fix up the guest room in the basement for me – like I wasn't a member of the family anymore, just someone crashing here for a couple of years until college, so why not drop me down below, out of sight?

And I didn't even have any time to get used to the idea of moving. Even though the baby was still months away from being born, Mom and Mike wanted me to change rooms as soon as possible.

"Because we need to decorate it as a nursery," my mom explained when I protested. "And because I can't paint while I'm pregnant, Mike will have to paint the nursery himself – so it makes sense for you to do your room now, while you're off for the summer and have time to do your own painting. Besides," she added, knowing she didn't quite have me yet, "there's always a possibility that this baby could come early."

I knew very well that the baby could come early – I'd heard enough about baby-making to know that if you have trouble getting pregnant in the first place, you might have more trouble making it all the way through nine months without something going wrong. Plus, my mom wasn't exactly young anymore. Part of me was actually thinking she shouldn't be making such a public display of her pregnancy – telling everyone, making me move out of my room and everything – until it was more of a "done deal." Like it was bad luck to be counting on it already. But I knew better than to challenge her or burst her bubble, so when she pointed it out, I just turned and left the room.

And I didn't talk about it with anyone – not even with my best friend, Ashley – for a long time.

Like I said, all of this happened just before I met Tyler. At the time, I knew that the new baby was going to be a huge change. But I had no idea how many other things in my life were about to shift.

Caitlyn's story continues in:

## Maybe Never, Maybe Now

by Kimberly Joy Peters / **978-1-897550-64-9**

In the sequel to the acclaimed novel, **Painting Caitlyn**, Caitlyn gets the opportunity to go on an exchange trip to Quebec, and wonders if this is her chance for a fresh start following a painful year. But soon, old fears and insecurities start to creep back in, and she second-guesses herself at every turn. As she embarks on a new romance, a figure from her past tries to make amends. Can Caitlyn find it within herself to trust again?

www.lobsterpress.com

## About the author:

**Kimberly Joy Peters**'s debut novel, ***Painting Caitlyn,*** was published by Lobster Press in 2006, and has been recognized by the International Reading Association, the American Library Association, the Maine Coalition to End Domestic Violence, and the British Columbia Teen Readers' Choice "Stellar Book" Awards. Kimberly followed ***Painting Caitlyn*** with ***Posing as Ashley,*** a novel about Caitlyn's best friend. It went on to win the Elementary Teachers' Federation of Ontario Writer's Award and was selected for the Canadian Children's Book Centre's "Best Books for Kids & Teens." Kimberly teaches French and art in Beaverton, Ontario, a town near the shores of Lake Simcoe. Visit her at www.kimberlyjoypeters.com.